The Sight Of Ali With A Baby In Her Arms Stopped Him Cold.

She was settling into the rocker with Joshua. The night-light bathed her in gold. Her tumbled curls, the shadows of her curves beneath her nightgown. His body reacted, his senses coming to swift attention. She shouldn't be having this effect on him, yet he couldn't tear his eyes away.

"I'll take him. Go back to bed." His tongue thickened on the words. *Back to bed.* They opened a floodgate of memories of what they'd shared. Of what he wanted to share with her again.

She looked up at him, and saw what he knew was reflected in his eyes. Hunger. Desire. Need.

A little voice in the back of his mind urged him to draw her into his arms, against his aching body. To do with her all those things his flesh clamored for.

Would he listen?

* * *

The Child They Didn't Expect
is part of the #1 bestselling miniseries from
Harlequin Desire—Billionaires & Babies: Powerful
men...wrapped around their babies' little fingers.

* * *

tell us what

D0583904

Dear Reader,

It never fails to amaze me how, in a huge wide world, you can always meet a compatriot while traveling abroad—especially when you come from a country as small as New Zealand. So sparked the idea for *The Child They Didn't Expect*.

As we all know, life can throw some wicked twists and turns at a person when they least expect it. Sometimes you think you're coasting along, all happy, and then the unbelievable happens to you or to one you love. And so it is for Ronin Marshall and Ali Carter in *The Child They Didn't Expect* when their idyllic holiday romance comes to an abrupt end with the sudden death of Ronin's sister and her husband.

Ronin is a strong, protective kind of guy, the one everyone can rely on in a tight or difficult situation, but suddenly becoming the guardian to his dead sister's baby is enough to throw him off his carefully crafted course and force him to reach out for some help of his own. Cue Ali Carter, a woman with a heart bigger than the ocean and a sad secret of her own. Can they overcome the roadblocks that life has thrown their way in an attempt to divide them, or can they both learn to love and open their hearts wide to a new future? You'll find out between these pages.

The Child They Didn't Expect is set in my home city of Auckland, New Zealand—a sprawling, bustling metropolis, fringed by the sea east and west and wide green belts of farm and lifestyle land north and south. A quarter of New Zealand's population lives within its broad-reaching borders. One of my favorite areas is not far from where I live— Whitford—so I took great delight in making Ronin's home there, and I hope you'll take great delight in visiting with him and Ali also.

Best wishes and happy reading!

Yvonne Lindsay

THE CHILD THEY DIDN'T EXPECT

—

YVONNE LINDSAY

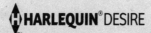

Recycling programs
for this product may
not exist in your area.

ISBN-13: 978-0-373-73343-9

The Child They Didn't Expect

Printed in U.S.A.

Books by Yvonne Lindsay

Harlequin Desire

Silhouette Desire

*New Zealand Knights
^Rogue Diamonds
¤Wed at Any Price
ΩThe Master Vintners

Other titles by this author available in ebook format.

YVONNE LINDSAY

New Zealand born, to Dutch immigrant parents, Yvonne Lindsay became an avid romance reader at the age of thirteen. Now married to her "blind date" and with two fabulous children, she remains a firm believer in the power of romance. Yvonne feels privileged to be able to bring to her readers the stories of her heart. In her spare time, when not writing, she can be found with her nose firmly in a book, reliving the power of love in all walks of life. She can be contacted via her website, www.yvonnelindsay.com.

I'm always very grateful to the generous hearts and minds that help me with the finer details of my books and this one is no different. This book I dedicate to Ashwini Singh with sincere thanks. Any errors relating to newborn intensive care are completely my own.

One

Ronin lay wide awake in the darkness, his body sated and relaxed, yet hyperaware of the woman sleeping in his arms—of the softness of her curves pressed against his skin, of the sound of her gentle rhythmic breathing. Her lush dark brown hair tickled his sensitized flesh but he didn't want to move from this place, lost as he still was in the intensity of their lovemaking.

He didn't do one-night stands. Not ever. Well, not until tonight. But there had been something about this woman—a fellow New Zealander—that had struck him from the moment he'd brushed past her in the beachfront restaurant of their hotel complex. An instant responsiveness he had never experienced before had stirred in him. Something that saw him agree to the restaurant hostess's suggestion that Ali join him at his reserved table after she was turned away due to overbooking.

The same something that had seen them go on to

dancing after dinner, and then to a walk on the moon-lit sands of Waikiki Beach. And finally, they had made love in her hotel room with a spontaneity and passion he'd never permitted himself to indulge in before.

His friends would be shocked if they ever heard that he—the king of all that was analytical and organized—had fallen into bed with a virtual stranger, purely based on *feelings* and the impulse of the moment. It wasn't his way, not at all. It flew in direct contrast to his talent for deductive reasoning, to his clinical efficiency in being able to take a problem apart and put it back together, to his ability to fix all things falling apart through logic and rationality. There had been nothing logical or ratio-nal about the night he had spent with this woman. And yet, it had been…magical. Yes, that was the only word he could think of to describe it—a word too ephemeral for his charts and numbers world.

Ali sighed and turned on her side, shifting away from him. He was about to reach for her, to pull her back and wake her so they could build on what they'd already savored together, when the discreet but persistent buzz of his cell phone from the pocket of his trousers, some-where on the floor, dragged his attention away.

He flicked a glance at the time on the digital dis-play across the room as he felt around for his trousers in the dark. 5:10 a.m. It definitely wouldn't be his client here in Waikiki who was calling. That only left home—New Zealand. His mind swiftly made the calculation. That would make it 4:10 a.m. tomorrow there, which was hardly a typical time for anyone to call. It was ei-ther a wrong number…or an emergency. He swept the phone into his hand, identifying his father's photo and number on the screen, and moved quickly to the hotel room bathroom.

Pulling the door closed behind him, he answered the phone. His father's anguished voice filled his ear.

"Dad, Dad, slow down. I can barely understand you."

"It's CeeCee, Ronin. She's dead. And R.J., too."

The horrifying words came through loud and clear. An icy cold sensation flooded through his veins. Surely this was some kind of nightmare. His beautiful and vibrant baby sister—dead? It couldn't be true. She'd been the picture of good health, blooming in late pregnancy, when he'd left home three days before. Ronin's brother-in-law had teased him about potentially missing the birth of his first niece or nephew because he'd been called to troubleshoot for an overseas client, yet again.

"How, Dad? When?" Shock made his lips stiff and uncooperative as he tried to form the words. "Tell me what happened."

"She went into labor. R.J. was driving her to the birthing unit. A drunk driver went through a red light. He hit them broadside, pushed them into a pole. They didn't stand a chance."

His father's voice cracked with emotion. The enormity of what had happened overwhelmed Ronin, and he felt his eyes burn with tears. As much as his brain screamed at him that this wasn't happening, logic dictated that this was real, actual, true. And here he was, in Hawaii, far from his family when they needed him most.

"The baby?" he managed to ask through a throat constricted by the clutch of raw grief.

"He was born by emergency caesarian. He nearly didn't make it. CeeCee died during the operation. Her injuries were too great for the doctors to save them both."

Amid excoriating pain that threatened to drive him to his knees, Ronin processed the news that he had a nephew and forced himself to grapple with the knowledge that the much-loved, much-anticipated baby was now an orphan. He dragged his thoughts together. "Is Mum all right?"

"She's in shock. We both are. I'm worried, Ronin. This isn't good for her heart. We need you, son."

"I'll be there as soon as I can. I promise."

He took some details from his father and then, telling him he'd be in touch as soon as he had flight information, he reluctantly severed the call. Leaning against the cool tile of the wall, he took in several deep breaths. Calm. He needed to be calm and organized and all those things that usually came to him as second nature. It was a tall order when all he wanted to do was weep for the senseless loss his family had just suffered. For the dreams his sister and her husband would never see fulfilled. For the child who would grow up without his parents.

When he felt he had himself under control, he slipped back into the hotel room and silently gathered his clothing from where he'd scattered it so mindlessly on the floor only a few hours before. He dressed as quickly and quietly as he could and then let himself out of the room with one thing and one thing only on his mind. He had to get home.

The flight back to New Zealand, via Brisbane in Australia, had been undeniably long. He could have waited for a shorter, more direct flight later that day, but he needed to be home *now* and this was the flight that would get him there first. Ronin had filled the time by making lists of what needed to be done when he arrived home, of people who would need to be contacted, the arrangements made. Through it all his heart ached with a pain that was not as easily compartmentalized as the lists and instructions he'd so assiduously written.

Finally, after fifteen-plus hours of travel and transit, he was back where he belonged—where he was needed most. He spotted his father's pale face in the Arrivals Hall the moment he stepped through from Customs. Strong, familiar arms clapped around him in a gesture that reminded him so much of when he was younger. And then he felt the shudder that passed through his father's body and knew the older man now needed his comfort far, far more than he'd ever needed his father's.

"I'm so glad you're back, son. So glad." His father's voice trembled, sounding a hundred years older than he'd been only a few short days before.

"Me too, Dad. Me too."

It was late, after midnight, when they drove from the airport to his parents' Mission Bay apartment. As they carefully traversed the rain-slicked roads, his father hesitating that extra few seconds as each red light turned to green, Ronin turned his thoughts back to the woman he'd left behind in Hawaii. He'd have to contact the hotel, to leave a message explaining where he'd gone. He'd been so focused on the task of getting home as quickly as possible it hadn't occurred to him until right now that he'd completely abandoned her.

When had she said she was traveling home again? He racked his memory but grief and exhaustion proved a barrier to his usually highly proficient brain. He made a mental note to get a message to her as soon as possible. But right now, he thought as they pulled into the underground parking at his parents' apartment building on Auckland's waterfront, his family—what was left of it—came first.

* * *

A touch of jet lag still weighed on her as Ali pulled up outside her business, Best for Baby. She knew she'd made the right decision to go to Hawaii for a vacation—it had been on her bucket list for years and she'd finally been able to tick it off. But she promised herself she'd be finding an airline carrier that offered direct flights at a more reasonable hour the next time she took the trip—cost be damned.

Of course it would have been more fun to share the vacation with someone else, but, in lieu of company, Ali had enjoyed the luxury of taking things at her own pace and being at her own beck and call for a change. Establishing her baby-planning business had taken everything out of her these past three years. She was proud of everything she'd accomplished, but it had taken a toll. She'd more than earned her holiday.

She should have returned reenergized and full of vigor. Instead, she was nursing emotional bruises that, logically, she knew shouldn't hurt quite as much as they did. It had been one night only. A handful of hours at best. She'd gone into it with no expectations, and yet she felt cheated, as if something potentially special had slipped from her grasp.

It was ridiculous, she knew. The confused pain she was experiencing was nothing like the pain she'd felt five years before, when her husband had admitted he didn't love her anymore, or even when he'd admitted to having an affair with the decorator he'd commissioned to redo his offices and to now loving *her*. But still, it left a sting when a guy sneaked out on a girl after the date night that, for Ali at least, had been the most excellent of all date nights—and especially when she'd broken every single rule in her book by sleeping with him. It had been an unpleasant shock to wake up alone. If he hadn't planned to see her again, why had he suggested they have breakfast in the morning and then spend her last full day in Hawaii together? Would it have killed him to leave her a message? Anything?

She gave herself a sharp mental shake. *Let it go, Ali,* she censured silently. *Let it go.* She'd suffered far worse and survived. This was a blip on her personal radar—no more, no less—and it was about time she treated it as such. She had to be practical about it. She didn't want another relationship—ever. Her business now filled the hole in her life that her broken marriage had left behind. Romance wasn't in the cards for her again. And she was fine with that. She should have known better than to let a little moonlight and a handsome stranger confuse matters. The entire experience now proved to her that she should never break her own rules about getting close to another guy, no matter how strongly she was attracted to him.

Satisfied she had her head on straight, Ali walked through the front door and called out to her assistant and good friend, Deb, at the front desk. "Good morning! Did you miss me?"

"Oh my God, yes. I've been flat off my feet. I have so much to tell you, but first you must tell me about Hawaii. Is it as beautiful as it looks in pictures?"

"It certainly is beautiful," she said with a smile. "Especially the sunsets. Here, let me show you."

Ali retrieved her cell phone from her satchel and opened the picture gallery. Together they oohed and ahhed over the shots she'd taken during the past week.

"Are you sure you didn't just photograph a postcard or something?" Deb asked dubiously as they lingered over a shot of the beach at sunset.

Ali looked at the screen of her phone, at the shades of apricot through to pink and purple that stained the sky and at the ubiquitous palm trees forming perfect silhouettes against it. That had been the night she'd met Ronin. The night she'd taken the plunge, thrown inhibitions to the wind and indulged in…well…*him*—the only man she'd ever slept with aside from her ex.

She vividly remembered everything about him from the first moment they'd brushed against one another. She'd just been turned away because the restaurant was fully booked, and as she was starting to leave, without looking where she was going, they had connected. She didn't so much *see* him, as get a series of *impressions* of him. The first, being his size. Not just his height exactly, but his bulk and presence. It was almost as if he wore his masculinity like a coat of armor, his strength and power as much a part of him as the cells that made up his body. The second impression was his scent. With the tangle of fragrances and aromas in the air the hint of his cologne had been a subtle contrast. Almost like the sea breeze that blew up the beach, yet with a cool freshness that tantalized and teased her senses.

Their arms had grazed one another with the lightest of touches, and her breath had caught in her chest. It had been so long since her body had reacted in that way—that buzz, that zing of total awareness—that she'd almost forgotten what attraction felt like, especially attraction on such a visceral level. She'd felt feminine in every sense of the word.

His voice had been deep and resonant as he'd excused himself and stepped away. Ali had remained silent, too stunned by her physical reaction to his touch to do any more than nod her acknowledgment of his apology. It wasn't until he was well past her that she'd realized his accent was just like her own—from New Zealand. She'd looked back over her shoulder and seen the hostess smile at him and pick up a menu before showing him through to his table. Beachfront. For one. And then she'd been invited to join him.

She shook off the flash of memory before her ever-astute friend saw too much on her face. Ali forced a laugh.

"Yes, I'm sure."

"And did you meet any hot guys? Please tell me you met someone."

She managed to summon a smile from somewhere. "I didn't go there to meet someone. I went there for a vacation, and that's exactly what I had. Now, tell me about what's kept you so busy while I was away," she finished, deflecting Deb's attention as effectively as she could.

Deb spent a good twenty minutes giving Ali the abridged version of what had been going on in her absence. Best for Baby, if requested, provided a range of services to expectant families, from baby showers to nursery shopping to interviewing and providing a shortlist of nannies, when needed. She'd had a slow start when she'd opened their doors three years prior, but over the past twelve months, referrals had begun to bring business with increasing frequency.

It was bittersweet work for a woman who knew she'd never bear a child of her own, but it was rewarding in its own way to create the perfect world for a new family.

A perfect world she'd never believed she wouldn't have.

As a child she'd been a little mother for all her toys. She loved children, and had always been eager to raise a house full of them—a dream that she had shared with her high school sweetheart, who had become her husband. They'd hoped to start building their family right away after their wedding…but it wasn't meant to be. Discovering she lacked the essential female ability to have a baby of her own had been a massive blow—one she'd believed she'd overcome with Richard at her side. But she'd discovered she was too flawed for him. So flawed that he'd stopped loving her—and eventually left her for another woman.

Over the past few years she'd become adept at hiding the pain her inadequacies caused her. As the youngest of four sisters, all of whom had children and had remained happily together with their spouses, it hadn't been easy, but she'd gotten there. Best for Baby had given her a sorely needed sense of purpose, and had gotten her through the worst of it.

"The Holden baby shower went really well. They loved the games, and the cupcakes," Deb said, pulling Ali's focus to the here and now.

"Did you send flowers to the bakery with our thank-you note? The way they pulled that together on such short notice really saved us," Ali said, remembering how, on the day of her departure to Hawaii, their usual catering supplier had let them down at the last minute.

"I certainly did. The owner called to say she'd be happy to continue to work with us in the future. Oh, and yesterday we got a new contract."

"Don't you mean a lead?"

"Nope. A bright, shiny new contract. Signed and everything."

"What? Just like that?" Ali asked in disbelief.

"Yup, just like that." Deb looked smug.

Usually there was a process—meetings with clients, presentations of proposals, acceptance of ideas and terms, etc. You didn't *just* get a new contract straightaway like that. Or at least she hadn't, up until now. Her incredulity must have shown on her face.

"Yes, I know. I was surprised, too, but there's some urgency involved as the baby has already been born," Deb said. "Because of complications he's still in hospital. The client wants the nursery completed before the baby is released to the family. And wait, there's more."

"How much more?" Ali asked, doubtful about this sudden good fortune.

"You have carte blanche on the nursery. Your design, your budget."

"No! Seriously? Are you certain this is legit?"

"Sure am. I emailed the contract to the client and it arrived back, fully completed and in duplicate, by courier the same day. Even better, the deposit landed in our bank account overnight."

Ali accepted the clipped papers that Deb handed to her and quickly perused them. Everything seemed to be in order. She looked at the bold signature at the bottom of the agreement. She couldn't make out the name, but it appeared a company rather than an individual had contracted Best for Baby's services. She hadn't heard of REM Consulting before, but that didn't mean anything.

"Well," she said on a slow exhalation of breath. "It certainly looks genuine."

"They want you to go around to the house, today if possible, and start putting things in motion. It doesn't sound like they have the vaguest idea of what they want, which is a bit weird, but they need the job done quickly. I told them you'd be there at three this afternoon."

Ali groaned inwardly. She'd hoped to spend all day in the office, catching up on email and correspondence, but it looked like some of that would have to wait until tonight. Oh well, it wasn't as if she had any grand plans for her evening, anyway. Work had been her constant companion in the past three years, so why should it be any different now?

"Okay, then. I'd better at least attempt to get up-to-date before I head out, hadn't I?"

"Lucky for you I left you a few things to do," Deb said with a cheeky smile. "I'll put the coffee on while you go through your email."

"Thanks, Deb. You're a lifesaver."

The morning passed quickly. Ali ate her lunch at her desk while checking job sheets for clients before heading out to her appointment. She'd made steady progress today, with Deb fielding her calls for her. With taking work home, by tomorrow afternoon, she'd be fully back on deck and up-to-date. She looked up at Deb as she came into her office.

"I called the client to confirm the meeting and I've checked the traffic report. The southern motorway is slow, so you might want to head out soon if you're going to make it to Whitford on time."

Ali glanced at her watch. "Thanks. I'll head out now."

It took nearly an hour for Ali to reach her destination, and she sent a silent message of thanks to Deb for giving her the heads-up to start driving early. She prided herself on punctuality but was prone to getting wrapped up in a project, so she sometimes needed that extra nudge. Once she left the motorway and headed into the green and rolling hills of the rural area on the fringe of the city, she felt herself begin to get excited about the task ahead.

This was the first time she had carte blanche to create everything from the floorboards up. Usually clients had pretty strong ideas already about what they wanted by the time they came to her, so it was a little odd that the parents didn't seem to have any preferences. But, she rationalized, if the baby was scheduled to remain in the hospital for another few days then he was likely premature. The parents might have thought they'd have more time to make a final decision. And now, maybe they were simply too busy with their new arrival to want to even think about such matters.

She wondered what business the baby's parents were in that they could afford both to live out here and to commission a job that would command a very high figure from Best for Baby. Well, whatever they did, Ali was committed to providing an exemplary nursery. Her GPS alerted her to the turnoff coming ahead and Ali slowed her car to take a right into the driveway. At the entrance she announced herself to the console and drove through as the verdigris iron gates gracefully swung open.

The driveway itself was long, more like a private road, she thought as she drove along it. Cows grazed in fields on either side of the gentle rise and she caught a glimpse of a couple of ponds with a few ducks floating happily on the surface. This really was idyllic. The child who grew up here would be lucky, indeed. The driveway curved up the rise to reveal the home she was visiting. It was difficult not to feel a pang of envy for the owners of the beautiful property that spread out before her. Constructed with a steeply sloping gray slate roof, the cream-toned brick house was both imposing and graciously subtle at the same time. She'd barely noticed it from the roadside, and yet from up here, it magnificently commanded an uninterrupted sweeping view right out over the Waitemata Harbor and out to the Hauraki Gulf.

Get with the program, she reminded herself as she parked her car near the front door. *You're not here to admire the scenery. You're here to do a job.* She gathered her things and got out of her car. An uncharacteristically nervous tremor passed through her at the prospect of meeting her new clients. Ali chalked it up to the unusual circumstances of the job as she rang the doorbell and then stood waiting in the portico, looking out at the expansive rural scene that spread before her.

Normally she'd have met with her clients at least twice before coming to their home. She liked to gauge how well they'd work together through preliminary meetings at her office before any contracts were signed. In a couple of cases, she'd even refused contracts because she'd known she wouldn't be able to get along with the people involved. This was such a personal business, everyone needed to be on the same page from the get-go. Would she get along with this couple? She hoped so. Her imagination fired to life as she waited, the natural setting and water beyond it already stimulating ideas for the nursery. It would be profoundly disappointing, and not just from a financial perspective, if she found she couldn't work with these clients.

Hearing the front door open behind her, she turned with a smile on her face. A smile that instantly froze in place as her eyes and her brain identified the person framed in the imposing entrance in front of her. As she recognized the stubbly jaw, the spikey dark blond hair, the intense blue gaze.

Ronin Marshall. Her one-night lover.

The last man on earth she'd ever expected, or now wanted, to see again.

Two

Ronin did a swift double take before his brain and his mouth kicked into gear.

"Ali?"

He'd heard the voice on the intercom at the gate but he'd been distracted, not really listening. Ali stood before him looking as poleaxed as he himself felt, but she seemed to gather herself together a moment later. Dressed in a salmon-pink rolled-collar blouse and pale gray pencil skirt, she was the epitome of professional chic. The color of her blouse did amazing things to her gently sun-kissed skin and made the soft gray-blue of her eyes stand out. Strange, he hadn't noticed what color her eyes were. Well, not so strange when he considered they'd met at night and most of what they'd done together after that had been by candlelight or no light at all.

"There must be some mistake," she said hesitantly. "*You* contracted our services?"

"Yes. Well, technically, my P.A. organized it."

"But you want a nursery," she stated.

"Yes, yes. Please, come in." He stepped back and gestured for her to enter the foyer. "I had no idea it would be you," he said involuntarily.

"Does that make a difference?" Ali asked pointedly, almost with a hint of challenge.

There was a light in her eyes that implied she was angry about something. It confused him. What on earth did she have to be so mad about?

"Of course not. I'm sure you're very good at your job. I just never expected to see you again. I tried to leave a message for you at the hotel, but you'd already checked out."

She raised one perfectly plucked brow in response. It was clear she didn't believe him. He sighed. Believe him or not, they'd have to put their feelings aside. They had a job to do, and he badly needed her help.

The funeral that morning had been harrowing and his emotions were still raw, his thoughts uncommonly scattered. Seeing Ali here, in his home, compounded that confusion. It'd been a hell of a day so far and, judging by the expression on Ali's face, it wasn't going to get better any time soon.

"Look," he said. "I owe you an apology. Can we please start again?"

He put out his hand. She hesitated a moment before grasping it. The second she did, he was instantly struck by that jolt of awareness he'd felt the first time he'd met her. Despite everything that had transpired since he'd left her bed, the connection between them remained.

He wanted to cling to it, to her. The notion was both atypical of him and utterly compelling at the same time.

"Please don't worry," she said. She pulled free of his clasp with a jerk. "Now, shall we get down to business?"

"Business." He nodded. So that was how she wanted to play it. To act like they'd never met before. To pretend that they'd never touched or kissed. That he had never been buried so deep inside her body that he'd begun to lose all sense of himself, instead reveling in her glory. Was it really possible for her to forget all that? He knew full well it wouldn't be possible for him.

If he hadn't seen the telltale flush of color that bloomed at the opening of her blouse when they'd shaken hands, he might have thought she'd been unmoved by their physical contact. But that hint of color, that evidence of the heat that had burned between them, told him far more than her demeanor. He was the king of compartmentalizing things. Of course he could play it her way. That didn't mean he'd like it.

"Come this way." He led her over the foyer's parquet flooring and turned right down a short hall. He gestured for her to go ahead of him into the slightly less formal living room, where he spent much of his leisure time while at home. "Please, take a seat. Can I get you something? Tea, coffee? A cool drink?"

"Just water, thank you," she said as she settled herself into one of the comfortable fabric-covered chairs arranged conversationally around the large wooden coffee table.

It only took a moment to grab a bottle of mineral water from the fridge and a couple of tumblers. He returned to the living room and poured water for each of them.

"I appreciate you being able to come out at such short notice."

"We pride ourselves on our service, Mr. Marshall," she said primly as she unfolded the cover from a tablet. A light touch of her fingertip and he saw the device come to life, much like he had not so very long ago beneath that very same touch.

"Ronin," he corrected.

They'd been intimate together—so deeply intimate. They might be discussing business, but he refused to sit there and listen to her call him Mr. Marshall.

She inclined her head but still avoided using his name. "Now, what is it exactly that you need from us?"

"Everything," he said.

For a moment grief and helplessness surged to the forefront of his mind, but he resolutely pushed the feelings back. He had to keep control of himself...but his usual cool rationality had never been so hard to reach. CeeCee and R.J.'s funeral had been hell in every sense of the word. It had made everything so real, so final. His parents had gone directly from the wake to the hospital. He'd wanted to go, too, but this meeting took precedence. He couldn't bring the baby home until he had something to bring him home to.

A ripple of fear rolled through the back of his mind. What if he'd bitten off more than he could chew with the decision to raise his nephew himself? For the briefest second he considered what his cousin Julia had said to him after the funeral. Already a mother of two, she and her husband had offered to bring CeeCee's son up in their family. It made sense, she'd said. She was already geared up for small children, and with her, her husband and her two daughters—both in primary school—the baby would have a wonderfully stable home. As she'd pointed out, being the infant's guardian didn't mean he had to actually raise him. He could still make sure the little boy had the best of everything without having him directly under his roof. With his long working hours, frequent travel and lack of a wife or committed girlfriend to share the load, Julia had claimed that Ronin's life simply didn't have room for a baby in it.

But it had been clearly outlined in CeeCee's and R.J.'s wills that they had wanted him to care for any children of theirs should anything ever happen to them. Ronin raised a hand to his eyes and swiped at the burning sensation that stung them. He owed it to his sister to fulfill her wishes. Besides, he'd assessed this from every angle already, and he was committed to seeing it through. And, as with any issue he troubleshot, that meant getting the right people in to help with the job. People, who in this case, had turned out to be Ali Carter.

He continued, "Look, I don't have the first idea of what to do."

"Then it's a good thing you called Best for Baby," Ali said, oblivious to the turmoil that was churning inside him. "So, correct me if I'm wrong. You have absolutely nothing here in preparation for the baby."

"That's right," he confirmed. "CeeCee was fiercely superstitious about buying anything before the baby was born. And she forbade anyone else from buying things. There wasn't even a baby shower, at her insistence. We tried to persuade her otherwise, but she was nothing if not determined."

A small frown flittered across her face so swiftly he wasn't sure he'd seen it. She drew in a deep breath and let it go slowly.

"And when is the baby coming home?"

"He should be released in about ten days' time, if all goes well."

She typed a note on her tablet. Even though she hadn't commented on the short time frame she had to work with, he had the impression she disapproved somehow. He knew his request was unusual, but this had mostly been covered in the contract, so he couldn't believe she was surprised by it. But then what was the problem? Maybe she was still angry with him for walking out on her in Hawaii. He had never been one to leave issues to fester. This thing between them needed to be brought out into the open.

"Look, Ali, about that night—"

She looked up from her note-taking.

"That night? Oh, you mean *that* night. Let's not talk about it shall we." She gave him a smile that was no more than a mere upward twitch of the corners of her full lips, utterly devoid of warmth. "I'd prefer it if we could confine our discussion to the task at hand."

Well, he'd tried. She didn't want to talk about it. That was just fine. A pity though, he thought, as his gaze followed the chain of silver beads that slipped inside the neckline of her blouse. He had a feeling that getting to know Ms. Alison Carter all over again would have been a very interesting exercise.

Ali focused on the ten-inch screen she held in front of her, building a checklist of all the things she'd need to tackle if she took this job on. She gave herself a mental shake. Who was she kidding—*if*? Best for Baby wouldn't and couldn't turn down this job. Deb had shown her the signed contract. They were bound to work with this…this *man*!

A near overwhelming surge of fury threatened to

break past her carefully controlled professionalism. How dare he cheat on his pregnant wife with her? How dare he cheat on his wife, period! Having been victim to an unfaithful husband herself, an affair with a married man was the last thing on this entire earth she would ever have willingly embarked upon. She'd rather die than be the other woman, than be the cause of the kind of pain and grief she'd gone through. Betrayal, on any level, was cruel—but this went several levels deeper than that.

Ali reached for her glass of water and took a long slug of the crystal clear liquid in an effort to tamp down the fiery anger that vied with sickening disgust deep inside her. *What a bastard,* she told herself. Yes, he was attractive. Even now her body, traitor that it was, virtually hummed with recognition, remembering his touch as if it were an imprint on her skin.

She drained her glass and set it back on the table with a sharp clunk. Attractive meant nothing whatsoever if it didn't come packaged along with a few other necessities to make up the man. Necessities like integrity, honesty and reliability—just to name the basics. Ali briefly closed her eyes and searched deeply for the inner strength she needed to get through this meeting as quickly and efficiently as possible. It galled her to even have to breathe the same air he was.

She pitied his poor wife, and the baby as well. They both deserved better. Ali quietly resolved to get this contract over with fast. She didn't want to find herself face-to-face with the new mother, not with the guilt she was now forced to bear, hanging like a yoke around her shoulders.

"Right," she said as she opened her eyes again. "Perhaps you could show me the room that will be the baby's nursery so I can take some measurements."

"Sure," Ronin said, his eyes never leaving her face as he stood. "It's upstairs. Come with me."

Ali rose to her feet and followed him from the room. As he ascended the staircase in front of her, she tried not to let her gaze linger on how the finely woven fabric of his trousers skimmed his taut behind, or to notice how the crisp fresh scent of his cologne subtly trailed in his wake. Every breath of him reminded her of the one sinfully exquisite night they'd spent together. Night? No, it hadn't even been that. It had been no more than a few hours, she reminded herself. And she wasn't entitled to reflect on the memory of those hours now that she knew the truth behind his oh-so-alluring facade. Ronin Marshall was a married man and, therefore, completely off limits.

"There are several bedrooms upstairs. The nannies will have the guest suite at the far end at their disposal. It's fully equipped with two bedrooms, a bathroom, a sitting room and a kitchenette."

Ali just nodded. It wasn't unusual for her wealthier clients to employ a nanny, although it definitely sounded as if he was talking in terms of more than one.

Ronin continued down the hall and pushed open the door into a spacious and airy bedroom. "I thought this room next to the guest suite would be best as a nursery."

She looked around, taking in the high-quality furnishings that already filled the room. "Do you want to keep anything that's already in here? The bed, perhaps?"

"Will the baby need any of it?" he asked with a helpless expression in his eyes.

Ali fought back the urge to sigh. Hadn't he paid any attention during his wife's pregnancy? Surely he should know the very basics of what their own child required.

"Not right away, no," she said, controlling her voice

so her disapproval wouldn't shine through. "I'd like to keep the bureau in here." She ran a hand over the provincial French chest of drawers. "But the rest can go into storage. The sooner the better, so I can get painters and paper hangers in here within the next couple of days."

"You have people who can come in that quickly?"

She arched a brow. "There are always people who can come in that quickly when the price is right."

He nodded. "That's good. I'll see to it that the furniture is out of here tomorrow. Do what you have to do."

"That's what you're paying me for," she answered, digging into her bag for her laser tape measure.

It only took a moment to record the dimensions of the room and the window. Together with the ideas she'd begun to dream up as she'd waited in the front portico her mind was brimming with enthusiasm. If only the client wasn't such a dirty, rotten, philandering creep, she'd be relishing this job. Instead, she couldn't wait to get back to the office and hand it off to Deb.

"Right," she said, with a brightness she was far from feeling. "I think that's everything. We'll be in touch."

"That's it?" he asked.

"For today."

"Okay, then." For a minute he looked nonplussed, but then his brow cleared. "Will you stay a while? Talk with me about the steps you'll be taking? I know I'm off to a late start, but I want to understand the task ahead, and what I can do to help it along."

"Mr. Marshall—" she started.

"Ronin. At least you can call me Ronin."

She pressed her lips into a line and sharply shook her head. "I need to get back and get the ball rolling on this so we don't waste any time."

"Look, I'm sorry I didn't leave you a message straightaway. I shouldn't have—"

"Please, that's not necessary. I'll see myself out."

She couldn't stay there another minute and hear his empty platitudes or even ponder at the gall of him to make them. Nothing would change the truth. She'd done the unthinkable—slept with a married man—and he'd done the unforgivable in betraying his wife, and making Ali party to that betrayal. Ali moved quickly out of the room and down the stairs. Behind her, Ronin's heavier tread was muffled by the carpet. He beat her to the door. With one hand on the ornate brass handle he faced her and offered her the other.

"Thank you for coming out. I do really appreciate you taking this on. Right now we have too many other things to focus on."

"Yes, well, this is what we're good at, so you can rest assured the baby will get the best of everything possible."

She steeled herself to take his hand, determined to keep their physical contact to a minimum. It made no difference. Palm against palm, their touch all but sizzled. She quickly pulled away and walked through the open doorway to her car. He stepped out onto the portico and watched her leave—not moving back inside, she noted through the rearview mirror, until she was a good distance from the house.

It was so unfair, she thought as she drove through the iron gates and turned left onto Whitford-Maraetai Road. How could he have been so...so *everything* and so nothing all at the same time? Clearly she needed to hone her inner lie detector some more. First her husband, now this guy. What kind of message was she inadvertently transmitting to the universe that caused her to attract men for whom fidelity was a negotiable bond?

She might never know the answer to that, she told herself as she whipped along the road back toward the motorway interchange. But there was one thing she definitely knew—and that was that Ronin Marshall, and men like him, had no place in her life.

Ever.

Three

Two days later Ronin pushed open the door to Best for Baby and decisively rang the silver-and-crystal bell at the abandoned reception desk. Abandoned, no doubt, because he'd been fobbed off with *the receptionist* while Alison Carter hid from him here at her office.

He rarely lost his temper. In fact, he was known for being cool under pressure. But this had made his blood boil and, as did everything involving Alison Carter from the moment he'd met her in Hawaii, it churned up emotions that were both unfamiliar and uncomfortable.

The soft noise of a door opening made him wheel around to face her. He didn't even give her a moment before he spoke.

"Why aren't you at my house?" he growled, fighting to keep his voice level.

For a split second she looked taken aback, but her

composure quickly settled back around her like an invisible cape.

"I sent my associate. Is there a problem?" she asked.

"Yes, there's a problem. Your lack of professionalism is the problem."

"My what? Are you complaining about the level of care my company is giving to your contract?" she answered, her face pale but resolute.

"I'm complaining that you're not doing the job yourself."

She squared her shoulders and lifted that dainty chin of hers a notch. "Deb has been with me since the firm opened, and she is equally capable of seeing to it that your nursery is completed on time."

"Deb's your receptionist, right?"

"Normally, yes," she answered, with obvious reluctance.

"And how many contracts has she undertaken that are as time-sensitive as this one?"

"This is her first, but I'm still supervi—"

"Not good enough."

"Your contract is with Best for Baby, not specifically with me," she pointed out in what was, to his way of thinking, a totally unreasonable *reasonable* voice.

But beneath her sangfroid, though, he heard the tremor of unease. It gave him power he wasn't afraid to use. Not when the ends justified the means. He wanted the best for his nephew, and that meant Ali Carter. If he had to make a stink to get her to handle his contract with her precious company personally, then a stink he'd darned well make.

"*You* will complete the contract with me, and only you."

Or else ominously remained unsaid.

"Are you threatening me?" she asked, her voice obviously unsteady now.

"Do I need to? Your firm promotes itself as doing what's best for baby. It's your name behind that promotion. If I'm not mistaken, doing what's best is the basis of your mission statement. Yes," he said in response to the look of surprise that flitted through her blue-gray eyes, "I've done my research."

"And your problem?"

Oh, she was good. He'd give her that. She'd pulled herself together, and if he hadn't already heard that weakness just a few moments before, he'd have thought she had the upper hand right now.

"My problem is that I contracted with your company with the expectation that I would receive the best, not the second best."

"I can assure you that Deb is as skilled and efficient as I am. In fact, she's probably better for this contract, as she has no reason on earth not to be. *She's* eager to work with you." She left the words "*I* am not" unsaid, but they echoed in the air around them nonetheless.

"So you admit that you're letting a personal issue stand in the way of your Best for Baby creed, as stated on your company website?"

"I…"

"Not terribly professional, is it?"

"I'm not compromising what my firm offers in any way by putting Deb on the contract."

"But she's not you. I want *you.*"

In more ways than one, he added silently. She picked up on the entendre, her cheeks draining of color before flushing pink once more.

"Well, we don't always get what we want, do we?" she snapped back.

"Give me one good reason why you won't work on this project yourself."

"A reason?" her voiced raised an octave. She let out a forced laugh that hung bitterly in the air between them.

"Is that so difficult?"

His words became the catalyst that broke the crucible of her control.

"Fine," she snapped. "You want my reason for not working directly with you, you can have it. Men like you who cheat on their wives and who expect the rest of the world to simply drop everything at their behest make me sick. Do you hear me? Sick! You're scum. You swan around an exotic location under the guise of work and you pick up stray needy women. You betray everything about yourself as a decent human being and all the promises you've made before heading home—without so much as a goodbye, I might add—to your perfect life and your perfect wife. *That's* why I won't work directly for you. Satisfied?"

A lesser man might have staggered under her onslaught. He was not that man.

"I'm not married," he said succinctly in the echoing silence that followed her unexpected tirade.

"Oh, and you think that makes it okay? Wife, partner—what difference does it make? You betrayed the mother of your child when you slept with me, which in my book makes you both a liar and a cheat."

Ronin tamped down his increasing anger, forcing his voice to remain calm. "I repeat. I am not married. Nor am I currently in any kind of romantic relationship. The baby is not my son. Legally, he's my ward."

"Your…your ward?"

Ali clutched at the lapels of her blouse with a shaking hand.

"He's my nephew. My dead sister's son." He sighed. Just saying the words ripped off the carefully layered mental dressing he'd been using to protect his emotional wounds. "Look, can we sit somewhere and discuss this like rational people?"

Ali let go of her blouse and gestured to the room behind her. "Please, come into my office."

Her heart raced as her mind played over the appalling way she'd just spoken to him. She never lost it like that, ever. Not to anyone, and especially not to a client. But this was just a little bit too raw for her. The first time since her divorce she'd trusted anyone enough to even consider kissing them, let alone sleeping with them, and this had happened. She could be forgiven for jumping to the wrong conclusion, but she couldn't be forgiven for the diatribe she'd just delivered. She'd be lucky if he didn't rip up their contract right now and throw it back in her face.

Two facts now echoed in her mind.

The baby wasn't his.

He wasn't married.

"Take a seat," she said, moving over to the carafe of iced water she kept on a credenza. She poured out two glasses and placed one on her desk in front of him. "Here. I know we both could probably do with something stronger, but it's all I have on hand."

"It's fine," he said. He reached for the glass and drained it with one long swallow.

"I apologize for jumping to conclusions, and for speaking to you like that," she said as calmly as she could. She settled behind her desk and looked at him directly. "And I'm deeply sorry for your loss."

Her eyes raked over him, taking in the shadows that

lingered under his eyes and the fine lines of strain that hadn't been on his face the first time she'd met him. She must have been too preoccupied to notice them when she'd seen him at his house the other day. He looked haggard, as if he'd been on the go non-stop.

"Thank you. It's why I had to leave you so suddenly the night we met. My father called to say my sister and her husband had been in a fatal accident. My nephew was born by emergency C-section immediately before his mother died. I left your room on autopilot. I wasn't really thinking clearly, I just knew I had to get home. By the time I realized how unfairly I'd treated you, I was already back here, and when I contacted the hotel, they said you'd checked out."

"I understand," she assured him, her heart breaking for the shock and pain he must have felt. She was close to her sisters and couldn't begin to imagine how she'd feel if the same thing had happened to one of them. "I would have done exactly the same thing."

He dipped his head in acknowledgment. "It's been hell this past week. So much to organize, so many people to see." He swiped a hand over his face. "And the baby. It would have helped if CeeCee hadn't been such a superstitious thing and had organized the nursery already. I could have simply transported everything to my house."

"Or stayed at theirs?"

"No," he shuddered. "That would have been too much. I couldn't."

"What about your parents? How are they coping?"

"They're devastated. The stress is playing havoc with my mother's heart condition."

Ali felt her heart break a little at the note of sheer anguish in his voice. She could tell he was holding on by a thread. Had he even had the chance to begin grieving himself?

"Oh, Ronin. I'm so sorry. If there's anything I can do, just name it."

"There is," he said, pulling himself together before her eyes. "Given the circumstances, you'll understand why I need you to complete the nursery. I don't want any mistakes or oversights. Everything has to be perfect."

She was about to point out that she wouldn't have put Deb on the assignment—with Best for Baby's reputation hanging on it—if she hadn't been confident that things would be done to his satisfaction. Instead, completely understanding how vital this all was to him, she murmured her assent.

"So you'll come back on the job?" he asked, lifting his head and looking straight into her eyes.

She could see the worry behind them and his concern that everything be perfect.

"Yes, but better than that, you'll have two of us for the price of one. Deb will continue to assist—for good reason," she clarified when it looked as if he might protest. "There is a great deal to be done in a very short time. Two heads will be better than one in this case. She's already coordinating the work crews. I'll get started on the nursery supplies and furniture tomorrow."

The tension that had gripped his frame from the moment she'd laid eyes on him seemed to slowly leach out.

"Good," he said on a harshly blown out breath. "Good. You know, I always imagined that one day I'd fill my house with a family. I just never thought for a minute it would happen like this."

He got up to leave and Ali rose with him. At the main door to her office he turned to her, composed once again.

"I'll be working from my home office tomorrow. Will I see you?"

Ali ran through a mental checklist in her head before giving him an affirmative nod. "Probably after lunch time. I'll bring some curtain swatches just to make sure we've got the right match with the walls."

"Fine. I'll key you in to the biometric reader at the gate and the front door so you can come and go as you wish."

She blinked at that.

"You'd trust me with that?"

"Why not? You aren't going to steal the family silver, are you?"

"No, of course not," she laughed in response.

"Then what's the problem? It'll be more convenient while you're coming and going in the next few days."

And, no doubt, it would ensure that it was her and not Deb going to the house, Ali thought after he'd gone. The idea wasn't unappealing—now that she knew he wasn't a dirty cheater.

He wasn't married. As the thought came back to her, she couldn't help it—an ember of longing flickered to life deep inside her once more.

As soon as Deb returned to the office, Ali explained she'd be back on the nursery outfitting as well. Her friend seemed unfazed about the change in seniority.

"Many hands make light work, and there's certainly plenty of work on this job to go around," Deb said, cocking her head to study her friend. "I get the feeling, though, that there's something you're not telling me."

Ali tried to hold her gaze and refute the underlying question on Deb's face but in the end she gave in.

"Look, I don't want to go into details, but long story

short, I met Ronin once a little while ago and we kind of hit it off, but nothing eventuated. Of course, when we got this contract and I saw him again, I assumed the baby was his and that he had been married when we first met."

"Oh," Deb said on a long sigh of understanding. "I get it. You must have been pretty mad, huh?"

"You could say that," Ali responded. Her stomach twisted sickly with the memory of how she'd spoken to Ronin earlier that day.

"But it's all sorted now, right?"

"It looks that way."

"So are you going to, y'know, see him again? And don't get all coy on me and say that naturally you'll see him in the course of the job. That's not what I mean, and you know it." Deb smirked and crossed her arms.

Ali shook her head slightly. Deb knew her too well. That was exactly what she'd been about to say. "No. We won't start seeing each other like that. He's just been through the wringer with the loss of his sister and her husband, and he has the additional pressure of keeping an eye out for his parents—not to mention the worry of the baby."

"Sounds like he needs a bit of distraction then, wouldn't you agree?" Deb said with a slow wink.

"I think distraction is the last thing he needs right now," Ali replied firmly, determined to close the subject. "Now, tell me, how did the paint finish turn out?"

They discussed the dove gray walls with white trim that had been painted that morning, and Deb showed Ali a couple of photos she'd taken with her tablet. Ali gave an approving nod at the contractor's work.

"They're fast and they're good, aren't they? We should pay a little over their premium for doing the job on such short notice. There's a large enough buffer in the budget for that, isn't there?"

Deb agreed, and they went on to check the list of items Ali had planned for her shopping expedition in the morning. They divided the lists. Deb was to purchase a diaper bag and supplies along with car seats—one for Ronin and one for the nannies—as well as a stroller and a portable crib in case the baby overnighted with his grandparents when he was a little older. Ali took on the nursery furniture and final decorations for the room, as well as the clothing and feeding necessities. She made a mental note to ask Ronin to check with the hospital about which formula the infant was being fed so she could make sure there was a sufficient supply at the house for when the baby came home.

By the time their working day drew to a close, she was feeling excited. It was because she would deeply enjoy the tasks ahead, she told herself firmly as she locked up the office and headed for her tiny apartment in Mount Eden. It had nothing to do with seeing Ronin again the next day.

Liar, she admitted to herself with an illicit thrill. Dressing the nursery was a fun job, but it had nothing to do with the slow moving heat that was spreading through her veins at the thought of being near him again. For all the words she'd bandied in Deb's direction today, she couldn't help but wonder—what would it be like if she and Ronin had another chance? Ali dismissed the question almost as swiftly as she'd thought it. She'd made her decision to remain single after the devastation her marriage had caused her. She didn't want or need the complications that a relationship with a man like Ronin Marshall would bring. Not one little bit.

Four

Ronin huffed in frustration as the doorbell rang for what felt like the hundredth time that morning. He'd had no idea how disruptive changing one room over for a tiny baby could be, but he was certainly finding out. He'd thought he could work quite comfortably at home but the steady stream of courier deliveries had negated that possibility. Now he had boxes strewn all over his foyer and no idea what was in them or where they needed to go.

"Feeling a bit under siege?" Ali asked with a sunny smile as he opened the door to her and she espied the stacks of boxes around him.

Relief seeped through him. Thank God she was there. *Now I might be able to put my focus where it belongs and get something done.*

"You could say that," he replied. "I could have done with you here from about ten this morning."

"I'm sorry. I came as quickly as I could." She hefted a book of curtain samples a little higher, and he swiftly reached out for the heavy item.

"Here, let me take that for you."

"Thanks. I have a couple more in the car."

"Seriously?"

She laughed at his obvious surprise and he felt his lips curl in response. "Yes, seriously. This is important."

She spun on a ridiculously delicate high heel and went straight to her car. Ronin followed and accepted the additional sample books from her, all the while trying to keep his gaze averted as the fabric of her neatly cut trousers pulled across the curves of her backside as she reached down into the trunk of her car. It occurred to him that nothing she wore stood out as particularly high fashion, yet everything still managed to deliver a punch when she put it on. He shifted his focus to the heavy books in his arms.

"All this for one set of curtains?" he asked.

"Oh, there were more," she answered with a sweet curve of her lips. "But they didn't have what I was looking for."

He followed her back into the house, where she paused in the foyer and inspected the labels on the various boxes that had accumulated there. She pulled her tablet out of her voluminous handbag and made some notes before stacking a couple of the smaller boxes in her arms.

"Shall we go upstairs? I'd like your opinion on the fabric swatches."

"Really, I know nothing about color. I usually left all that to…" His voice tailed off as that sweeping sense of loss tugged hard at his heart.

Decorating had been CeeCee's forte and her business, and she'd been exceptional at it. It was part of the reason he'd teased her so mercilessly about not doing anything for the baby's room. She'd never been superstitious growing up, which begged the question—had she had some intuition that something was going to go wrong? He shoved the idea from his mind before it could bloom into something further. He'd never held with that way of thinking and never would. To him intuition was, more accurately, picking up subconscious clues. No clue on earth could have predicted what would happen the night CeeCee and R.J. were killed.

He realized that Ali was waiting for him to finish his sentence. "To others who are far more adept at it than I am," he finished lamely.

"Well, if you're happy for me to make the final choice, I'm okay with that. I just thought that since it's your home we're working on you might like some input."

"I'll take these up for you and leave you to it. I have a conference call with a client in Vietnam shortly that should take about an hour. Please don't leave until I'm done. I really can't afford any delivery interruptions during the call, so if you could take care of opening the gate and getting the door, I would really appreciate it."

Ali smiled calmly. "No problem at all. I'll be here all afternoon. The furniture will be delivered by three, and I'd like to set it up as quickly as possible."

"Good, I'll get your fingerprint programmed into the biometric reader when I'm finished on the call."

They went upstairs and Ali pushed open the door to what was to be the nursery. Ronin was a little surprised at how much had already changed. He'd gotten his two part-time groundsmen to remove the furniture and store it in the loft above his multicar garage, together with the carpet square that had been in the room. Last time he'd looked in, the wooden plank floorboards had been covered with paint-spattered drop cloths and the walls had been a patchwork of the original off-white with an array of softer lemons, blues and grays. He was pleasantly surprised by the solid block of pale but warm gray that now covered the walls, offset by pristine white-painted trim on the deep skirting boards and the window frame.

"I wasn't sure what you'd decided on in here, but I have to say I like it," he said, laying the stack of curtain books on the floor.

"It looks great, doesn't it? Initially I'd thought to go with the pale blue on three walls and then to have a farm scene mural painted on one wall, but you only need to look out the window to appreciate that view more than anything that could be painted in place. Deb and I decided the gray was best and would work as baby grows older, too. Removable borders can provide features anyway, and they can be changed more easily, too."

Ronin tried to envision what she was talking about, but it all went right over his head. He was far more comfortable talking specifications and load-bearing structures than he was visualizing what was obviously so clear in her head.

Ali bent and rummaged through the fabric samples, extracting a sheer white gauze and then flipping back and forth through each of the other books. Their samples were, to his eye at least, much the same color as the nursery walls.

"Here," she said, holding one book open to a self-patterned fabric swatch a couple of shades darker than what was already on the wall. "Could you hold that up for me over by the window? I want to see how it works with the rest of the room."

He did as she bid and was surprised to see her shake her head vehemently. "What? Wrong color?"

"Totally," she muttered, digging back through the samples again. "Here, try this one."

To him they looked identical, but he dutifully held the sample up for her.

"Yes, that's better," she said, tilting her head slightly to one side and taking a step back. "In fact, I think that's perfect. We'll put the drapes against the window with the sheers on the bedroom side. That way the sheers will soften the effect on the whole room when the drapes are closed."

"I know what you're saying should make sense," he laughed. "But it sounds like a foreign language to me."

Her face broke into a wide smile and she gave him a cheeky wink. "Then it's a good job you hired Best for Baby, isn't it?"

She looked just as she had when they'd talked over the dinner table in Hawaii. He'd been reluctant, after a taxing day with a client, to share his solitude. But when the restaurant hostess had requested he allow someone she'd had to turn away to join him, and had pointed Ali out in the bar, he'd recognized her as the woman he'd brushed against in the crowded restaurant lobby. The woman who'd unwittingly triggered a startlingly visceral reaction. His initial resistance had been demolished and he'd said yes.

He wanted that again. That carefree easiness between them. That sense of being on a voyage of discovery together.

"Ali—" he started, taking a tentative step toward her. "Yes?"

God, he wanted nothing more than to take her in

his arms and kiss her. To revisit that exquisite oblivion they'd shared the night they met.

"I—" He broke off with a muttered expletive as his phone chirped in his trouser pocket. He identified the number of his office on the screen. "I'm sorry, but I need to get this."

"No problem. I'll be around here or downstairs if you need me."

She took the sample book from him, and as she moved away again he caught the fresh floral sweetness of her perfume. It was so subtle he was unsure he'd even smelled it at all, but it had a very immediate effect on his body. Need bloomed low in his groin. The phone in his hand continued to chirp. He forced his attention away from the woman who'd ensnared him and fought his libido under control. This kind of thing didn't happen in his normally rigidly structured world. Yes, he knew desire—what man didn't? But he'd never known it like this.

He barked a greeting into his phone. Walking from the nursery, he forced himself not to wonder why each step away from Ali felt as if it were a mile rather than a mere yard.

Well, that was intense, Ali thought as she watched Ronin leave the room. For a moment there she'd thought he was going to close the gap between them and kiss her. His eyes had darkened to a deep denim blue and fixed on her, as if the world had narrowed to only contain the two of them. Her heart still thumped in her chest, pumping blood to her extremities and heightening her awareness to a fever pitch.

She bit down on her lower lip. A lip that tingled in anticipation of his caress. A lip that mourned the caress that hadn't happened. Obviously their initial attraction was still there just as strongly as it had been an entire hemisphere away—their more recent contretemps notwithstanding.

She closed the sample books and stacked them on one side of the room. It was getting more difficult every time she saw him to remind herself she didn't want to go there again—that she was totally wrong for him. She had to stay professional. He was her client and she was contracted by him to do a job—a job that involved a helpless, parentless infant. Something deep inside her ached at the thought. What she wouldn't give to be that parent—to be that special someone to nurture and raise and love the child.

When she'd discovered she couldn't bear children of her own, she'd imagined that she and her husband would adopt, but he'd been opposed to the idea. She had thought he just needed a while to adjust to the idea of their dreams taking a different shape. She'd tried to give him space and time—space and time he'd used to go behind her back and fall in love with the woman he'd left her for. His lover had represented a new start for Richard, a second chance on the path to the life he'd planned…while Ali was clearly nothing more to him than a dead end.

It had been a painfully hard lesson to learn. Never in their years of courtship, or their marriage, had he even intimated that his love for her was contingent on her ability to produce and raise a family with him. That knowledge had been even more hurtful than the news that she was infertile.

Infertility was something they should have been able to deal with together. Thousands of couples the world over did every day. While she'd railed against the unfairness of it all—especially when faced consistently with evidence of her three sisters' abundant fertility and happy marriages—it had been her husband's rejection of *her*, and his twisted belief that it somehow reflected on him as a man, that had been her undoing. Those scars still ran deep—still made her feel vulnerable and inclined to withdraw from placing herself in that position a second time.

She reminded herself she was not, and probably never would be, ready to put herself out there again. There was no way she would run the risk of being rejected again. Hadn't she learned her lesson? She'd already felt dreadful when Ronin had seemingly abandoned her after their night together. What if they did get together and he did let her down again?

"Talk about getting ahead of yourself," she muttered to the empty space around her. "Very shortly he's going to be incredibly busy raising a child. He certainly won't have time for you. Nothing's happened and nothing will happen."

But there was a piece of her that *wanted* something to happen, that wanted Ronin Marshall with an ache that went deep down to her core.

Ali busied herself over the next few hours unpacking the boxes that had been stowed in the foyer. Some of the items needed assembly, so she retrieved her tool kit from her car before kicking off her heels and starting to put together the change station and the crib. After a short time, even without all the finishing touches, the nursery began to look like a baby's room. Just doing this, creating a safe and loving haven for someone else's unknown child, filled the echoing hollow inside her. Even if only briefly. It was why she loved doing what she did.

A sound at the door made her look up from where she was kneeling on the floor, reading the final instructions on the change station. Heat flushed her skin when she saw Ronin. She scrambled to her stocking feet, only to feel at a disadvantage as he towered over her.

"Is everything going okay here?" he asked, his eyes scanning the room.

"Pretty much," she said. "I just need a step ladder to put this mobile up over the crib. I can bring one out tomorrow, unless you have one here I can borrow?"

"There's one in the garage. I'll get it for you."

"Great. After that's up I'd best head off. I need to stop at the office and clear messages with Deb."

"Must you?" he asked, his brows pulling into a straight line. "I was wondering if you'd like to join me for an early dinner. I thought we could go down to Pine Harbor and eat there. There's a nice place overlooking the marina."

"Dinner?" she repeated, startled.

"Yes, you know, that meal people have in the evening some time before they go to bed?"

She laughed, but even so she felt her breath hitch just a little. Here it was. An overture. She should make it clear the only thing between them was a professional relationship, and turn his offer down. Really, she should. Hadn't she just been having a major internal discussion about this very issue? She'd say no, and that would be that. Simple.

"I'd love to," she said with a smile.

Five

Ali found the drive to the marina in Ronin's car too short and too long at the same time. She could barely keep her eyes from his long, capable fingers wrapped casually on the leather-covered steering wheel, nor push away the memories that flooded her mind of how those fingers had felt as they'd explored her body. Memories that left her breath shallow, an unignorable sensation tingling at her core.

When they pulled into the parking lot she dragged her eyes and her awareness to her surroundings and an involuntary exclamation of delight escaped her. The marina glowed in the early evening sun. The palm trees that bordered the road suddenly reminded her of another sunset, another dinner shared with this man…and what had come after.

"It's pretty here," she said, squirming a little in her seat.

"It is," he agreed, getting out of the car and coming around to open her door.

He offered her a hand and she took it automatically. Again she felt that electric sense of awareness at his touch. *Will this never stop?* she wondered. A part of her really didn't want it to, but then the other part, the fragile broken part of her mind and her heart, craved protection and set up a new caution in her mind.

Not letting go of her hand, he led her toward one of the buildings. They took a seat at the window, looking toward the ferry landing, where passengers—most of them from Auckland's city center, by the looks of it—were disembarking a vessel.

"This is such a lovely setting," she commented after the waitress took their drink orders and left them to peruse the menu. "I had no idea this place existed. Thank you for inviting me."

"Thank you for joining me."

She studied him a moment. "Why did you ask me to dinner?"

"Isn't it obvious?" he replied, his eyes doing that thing where they darkened to denim again.

Obvious? Did he feel the same attraction she felt? "Perhaps you need to explain."

Ronin leaned forward, one hand playing with the condensation on the side of his glass as he chose his words with obvious deliberation.

"I'm not normally an impulsive man, Ali. But there's something about you that makes me want to throw all my caution to the wind. To be with you."

"Oh," she uttered, her eyes widening in shock. Of all the things he could have said—the polite conversation she'd expected—that was probably what she'd least expected to hear.

"Too much?" he asked with a quick grin that crinkled the corners of his eyes and lifted most of the strain she'd become accustomed to seeing there.

"Maybe," she hedged. Even as she did so, her pulse leapt in response to the intensity reflected in his gaze.

"The way I see it is this. We jumped over several vital steps in the getting-to-know you stages of attraction when we met in Waikiki, and then I ran out on you without explanation. I figure we didn't really have the opportunity to get off to the right start, and I'd like to remedy that."

The waitress returned with their drinks, interrupting him for a moment.

"Are you ready to order?" the waitress asked brightly.

"Just a few more minutes, please," Ronin replied. The moment she was gone, he turned the intensity of his attention back to Ali. "I think we should start over. Get better acquainted. What do you think?"

"I..." Ali searched for the right words to say. Regret at her impulsive acceptance of his dinner offer pounded through her brain. Hadn't she just been telling herself she didn't want a relationship? It was time to draw a line in the sand. To make it clear to Ronin exactly where her boundaries were. "Look, please don't take this the wrong way, but I really don't think that's a good idea. What happened when we met, I'm not like that. I mean, I don't usually—"

"Me neither," he interrupted, picking up the glass of Central Otago Pinot Noir he'd ordered. "That's exactly my point. Clearly there's something here—something that made both of us willing to take a chance. Don't you think the chemistry we shared is worth exploring some more?"

"Look, Ronin, I—"

"Just think about it. A new beginning." He held his drink toward her in a toast. Automatically she lifted her lemon lime and bitters and allowed him to clink his glass against hers. This was wrong and yet so incredibly tempting at the same time. She already knew they struck sparks off one another—sparks that would make it far too difficult for her to keep a clear head. If she gave in to the attraction between them, she wouldn't be able to stay detached. She'd fall too hard, too fast and far too deep to be able to pull herself back out without pain. If she had an ounce of sense left in her mind she'd be hightailing it out of there as fast as she could.

Clearly that last ounce had departed.

Tomorrow she'd make it clear that theirs couldn't be any more than a client/contractor association. She just had to hope that would be soon enough.

They studied their menus. Ali asked Ronin for his recommendations, since he was a regular. When the waitress came back, they were ready. After she'd gone, Ali looked up to find Ronin watching her.

"What?" she asked. "Have I got lipstick on my teeth or something?"

"No," he laughed. "I was just calculating what the odds were of us meeting up again like we did."

"Pretty slim, I would have thought. It certainly wasn't a good thing that reintroduced us," she said, with a pang in her heart for the loss his family had undergone.

"No, it wasn't."

"Was your sister your only sibling?"

He nodded. "I still struggle to believe she's gone."

"How's the baby doing?" Ali asked, wishing suddenly that she hadn't chosen this track of conversation, but feeling committed now she'd started it.

"He's holding his own. Getting a little stronger every

day. They're trying to establish feeding so he can come home. We each try to spend time with him at the hospital, my mum and dad and I, so he'll be used to us when he comes out." A strangely bemused expression settled on his face.

"What is it?" Ali asked, concerned.

"Since he's been in the Newborn Intensive Care Unit, they've encouraged us to be there as much as possible, and to hold him even though he's been ventilated. Last night, when I went to see him, he was off the ventilator. The nurse told me about kangaroo cuddles."

"Kangaroo cuddles? I haven't heard of those."

"It's chest-to-chest, skin-to-skin contact. You sit in an easy chair and the nurse lays the baby on your bare skin." Ronin's eyes became unfocused for a moment, as if he was lost in the memory. "It's weird, but it's like he knows he's coming home to me. He was fussy when she first picked him up, but as soon as she laid him on me and covered him with a blanket, he gave this little sigh and settled right into my chest."

"That must have made you feel special," she said softly.

"Special? I don't know. He's so small. So dependent. It's kind of terrifying."

Ali felt tears sting her eyes. To hear this big, strong man admit his fear of caring for and raising his nephew tugged at her heart. "He's so lucky to have you."

His gaze returned to its usual sharpness. "He'd have been better off with his parents."

"I know, but at least he has you and your mum and dad, who care so much about him. What about his other grandparents. Are they around?"

"No, R.J.'s parents died some time ago apparently, and he was an only child."

"It must be hard for you all."

"It is, but we still have the baby. To have lost him too would have been the final blow for my mother, I think." He took another sip of his wine and looked out the window for a while before returning his gaze to her. "What about you? Brothers? Sisters? Parents still around?"

Ali latched on to the change in subject. "Oh, I have three sisters, all older than me. All married with families. Mum and Dad complain they never get a weekend to themselves because they're always having one lot of grandkids or another, but, just privately, I think they love it. They wouldn't have it any other way."

"Must make family gatherings fun," Ronin said, with another one of those heart-stopping grins.

"They're busy, that's for sure."

"And you? Is coming from a big family part of the reason you do what you do?"

Ali had been hoping the conversation would not lead in this direction, but she was well practiced at diversion. "Well, I certainly had plenty of experience helping my sisters prepare for my nieces and nephews," she said with a forced laugh. "But, I guess I was at a crossroads in my life and I figured there was a gap in the market here for something like that. I'd heard of party and other types of planners here, but when I heard about baby planners in the States, I decided that was what I wanted to do. After some research I did exactly that and started the company."

The summary didn't do justice to how hard she'd had to work to establish her business, or all she'd had to sacrifice. Most of the money she'd received in the settlement when her marriage had been dissolved—after their requisite two-year separation—had been poured into Best for Baby. She'd only kept back enough to pay for six months of living expenses and the lease on her apartment—against her parents' urging that she move back home with them until she was securely on her feet. She had trusted in her ability to earn enough to make the monthly payments and to live after those first six months.

There had been times when she'd wanted to crawl away from it all and to stay wrapped in the cocoon of safety her parents had offered. But with the failure of her marriage and her own perceived failure of herself as a woman still so sharply painful, she knew she had to reach out for herself, to rebuild her life, or give up all together.

"What about you?" she asked of Ronin, eager to turn the focus of their conversation back to him before he probed too deeply into her past. "What is REM Consulting?"

"We're a civil engineering company, and we consult on international projects. Mostly major building sites and complexes. My role is mainly as a troubleshooter. Generally I try to prevent the bad things from happening, handle risk management, that kind of thing. When things go wrong and solutions need to be found fast, I get called in to put everything right again."

She thought about how swiftly he must have had to move when he'd received the news about his sister and her husband. Having that background probably helped him remain calm and controlled in a situation that would most likely render others incapable of logical thoughts.

"Does your work take you away often?" she asked.

He nodded. "And usually at very short notice. It's why I'll need a rotation of nannies at the house. You got the brief on that, didn't you?"

"Yes, I did. I've got Deb compiling a list of suitable

applicants for initial interview. You mentioned you preferred nannies with nursing experience. Those skills will come at quite a cost. You do realize that?"

He made a sweeping movement with one arm. "Cost isn't an issue. My nephew's well-being is all that matters."

It struck Ali that while Ronin was doing all he could both physically and materially for the newborn, she still had questions about the baby's emotional support system. Ronin was clearly confident when it came to providing for his nephew, but was visibly nervous at the thought of nurturing the baby. While her family life had been loud and chaotic with six of them crowded into a small three-bedroom bungalow in the suburbs, her upbringing had been a happy one, with love and affection showered on Ali and her sisters by parents who put their children first.

And then there was Ronin's work. With him being on call for a wide range of clients all over the world, how consistent would things be at home? It was impossible for him to be a full-time father, with all the loving care that should entail, even if he wanted to.

"When will you be available to interview the shortlist of nannies?" she asked, forcing her thoughts back to her tasks.

"It'd probably be best if I see them in my office in town. I'll check my diary and call you with dates in the morning."

She'd have to be satisfied with that for now, she decided. No matter her own thoughts on the situation, the baby's emotional care wasn't her responsibility, and besides, Ronin was doing his best to step up to his duty to the baby. It wasn't her place to pry, beyond the scope of her job.

Their meals arrived and they turned their attention to the food. As the sun lowered over the western horizon, their conversation drifted away from what were, for Ali at least, work-related matters, and onto more personal interests. By the time they finished coffee and dessert they'd found a mutual love of English crime novels and old black-and-white movies.

Ali flicked a glance at her watch and sighed regretfully. "As lovely as this has been, I'm really going to need to head home."

"You could stay with me," Ronin offered without hesitation. "I have several guest rooms. You're welcome to use one, if you prefer."

If she preferred? Her imagination set her synapses firing.

"Oh, no, I don't think that's a good idea, but thank you for the offer," she answered with a twist of her lips. As if she could sleep under the same roof as him and not replay in her mind over and over what they could be enjoying together. She had enough trouble in her own bed in her tiny apartment. "I need an early start at the office tomorrow before another round of shopping and then the preliminary interviews for your nannies."

If he was disappointed in her response, he hid it well.

"Will I see you out at the house tomorrow?" he asked.

"No, not tomorrow, but I'll be back first thing the day after."

"I'll make sure I'm home. We can do lunch together."

"I *am* supposed to be working when I'm at your house," she reminded him with a small frown. "I take my obligations seriously."

"As do I," he answered, his face an implacable mask all of a sudden. He leaned forward and took her hand.

"Besides, as your current employer, surely it's my duty to make sure you have all your breaks?"

She couldn't help but laugh. "Okay, lunch together sounds nice. Thank you."

Ronin studied the figures on the estimate for the new project in Southeast Asia. It was the third time he'd applied himself to the document today—or at least attempted to apply himself to it. But he couldn't make himself concentrate. Giving up in frustration, he pushed his executive chair back from his desk and swiveled around to face the sparkling Waitemata Harbor. Even so, he didn't notice the spectacular view. His thoughts were elsewhere, far away from his office.

It wouldn't take a rocket scientist to figure out why his thoughts were so fractured, why his legendary control was so off-balance.

Alison Carter. Just picturing her in his mind was distraction enough, let alone remembering the night they'd shared in Hawaii. That night before his world imploded. He raised a hand to rub wearily at his forehead. So much had happened in the past few weeks, and he'd had so little power over any of it. His life had changed, and even though he was holding on to whatever he could, with a grip that was becoming more tenacious every second, he felt as if he was losing self-control. He couldn't afford to fall apart, not with everyone depending on him—and sometimes the weight of keeping everything together bore down on him more heavily than it should.

But Ali? She was a beacon in the darkness. A reminder that life did go on. And for some reason just being around her calmed him. Well, he admitted with a rueful smile, maybe *calm* wasn't quite the word he was looking for, not when his body reacted the way it did at the simple thought of her. Normally, he'd have worried about the strength of his response to her, the way she could push all other thoughts out of his head. Even the most passionate of his relationships in the past had never made him feel the way Ali had in just one night. Feelings that intense, especially on such a short acquaintance, should have seen him stepping back. But he couldn't step back from Ali, not when just being around her was enough to make the weight of his grief and his responsibility fade. Surely there was no harm in indulging in that pleasure for just a little while longer.

He looked forward to seeing her again the next day, to treating her to lunch and getting to know her a little better outside of her efficient capacity as a baby planner.

His eyes focused on the harbor now, giving him an idea for what they could do for their lunch date. He spun his chair around and punched the speaker to talk to his P.A. in the office outside his.

"Maeve? Can you get me a list of restaurants on Waiheke that have helipads?" he asked.

"Restaurants. Waiheke. Helipads. I'll get back to you shortly, Mr. Marshall," his scarily efficient P.A. replied in a smooth tone.

His mother's age, Maeve was one of those miracles of efficiency who made his job and quite frankly his life much simpler—even if she was old-school enough to insist on calling him Mr. Marshall and not Ronin, as he'd asked. As good as her word, Maeve was in his office ten minutes later with a printed list of restaurant names, website links, phone numbers and addresses, together with GPS coordinates. A perfectionist himself, Ronin appreciated her attention to detail.

"Is that what you wanted?" she asked as he scanned

the list, his eyes alighting on the name he was looking for.

"Perfect," he said, looking up. "Thanks."

"Did you want me to make a booking for you?"
Maeve began to turn to leave his office.

"No, I'll handle this myself."

Her step faltered on the carpeted floor. "Yourself?"

He looked up, meeting her surprised expression. "I
do know how to make my own restaurant bookings,"
he said drily.

"You might know how, but you never do it. This
isn't work-related—it's personal. You've met someone,
haven't you?" she asked, her eyes alight now with cu-
riosity.

Maeve had worked for him for five years, and they
were a well-oiled machine. He'd never known her to
ask an intimate question before. In fact, aside from the
facts that she was unmarried and shared a rambling old
Kauri villa in Epsom with her mother, he knew very
little about her personal life, either. He raised an eye-
brow at her and her expression sharpened.

"Don't bother giving me that look," she said sternly.
"Everyone around here knows you eat, sleep and dream
work in your downtime. If you even *have* downtime.
I think it's good that you have something other than
work to look forward to in your life. Especially now.
Life..." She hesitated a second or two, as if trying to decide whether or not she should continue before taking
a deep breath and forging on. "Life is too precious to
waste a moment or to let it pass you by. Everyone needs
balance. It's past time you found yours."

"You think I'm unbalanced?" he asked, deliberately
misconstruing her comments.

She made a sound of irritation that made him feel

like nothing more than a difficult child. "Don't twist my
words, Mr. Marshall. You know exactly what I mean."

Chastened, he gave her a half smile. "Yes, it is personal, and I'll handle the booking myself. Thank you for
the information, Maeve, I appreciate it. Oh, and could
you book the helicopter for me for three hours tomorrow afternoon from one o'clock?"

"Consider it done," she said, her smile making her
look ten years younger. "And I meant what I said about
not wasting a moment. If she's special, you make sure
you don't let her pass you by."

"What makes you so sure a woman is involved?" he
asked, testing her knowledge and insight into him just
that little bit further.

"Oh, please. If it wasn't a woman, those estimates
would be back on my desk by now, even with all you've
been through these past two weeks," she replied archly.
"It's a woman, all right."

Ronin watched in wonder as Maeve left his office,
closing his door behind her. He weighed her words carefully. She was right, as she always was, he conceded.

Ali truly was a distraction from his work—a distraction that he never would have tolerated before. But
somehow he couldn't bring himself to mind too much.
With all he was handling, it might seem like now was
the worst possible time for any diversions, but instead
Ali was exactly what he needed—someone to pull him
away from it all, to restore him for the challenges that
still lay ahead. For once, he wouldn't focus on the big
picture. He wouldn't make contingency plans, or find
an exit strategy. He'd just take this unexpected source
of pleasure that had fallen into his life right when he
needed it most, and enjoy it while it lasted.

He ran his finger down the list of restaurants and

stopped on one, then lifted the handset of his phone to make the lunch booking.

When Ali arrived at Ronin's house, her car loaded with supplies for the nursery, he was waiting on the front porch for her.

"Looks like my bank account is getting a hammering," he commented as he helped her carry several bags and boxes from the car.

"Looking after a little one isn't cheap, and you did say you wanted the best of everything," she pointed out.

"I would never settle for anything less."

Upstairs, she exclaimed in delight as they entered the nursery. "Oh, the carpet square arrived. What do you think?"

"Am I supposed to think anything of it? It's carpet."

"That's such a male response." Ali chuckled as she slipped out of her shoes and let her stocking feet sink into the thick gray-and-white-patterned square she'd ordered for the room several days before. "Take your shoes off and feel it," she urged.

Throwing her a quizzical glance, Ronin did as she requested.

"Doesn't it feel divine?" she asked him.

"It feels like carpet." When she cast him a disparaging look, he shrugged. "I can't help it. I'm an engineer, not a decorator. That was more my sister's forte than mine. She did most of the house for me."

She'd done a lovely job of it, too, Ali thought. Even though the property could easily grace the pages of a home decorating magazine, it still had a homelike feel about it. As if you could just curl up on a couch in the living room and read a book without worrying about leaving marks on the furniture or flattening the cushions.

"She certainly had a knack for it," Ali commented. "Right, well, I need to unpack these things and put them away, and then I'll be ready for that lunch you promised."

"I hope you'll enjoy it. I've got something special planned," he said enigmatically as he left her to her own devices.

What did he mean by that? she wondered as she stacked packets of newborn diapers on the shelving in the cupboard. It was lunch, for heaven's sake. How complicated could that be? The only way she'd find out would be to finish her morning's tasks, she told herself, dragging her thoughts back to where they belonged. It was time to apply herself to the work in which she took so much pride.

Ali extracted a selection of babywear, which she'd hand-washed, from one of the carry bags she'd brought upstairs, and placed the clothing carefully into the chest of drawers against the wall. Once done, she looked around her. Her gaze alighted on the sheep mobile hanging above the crib, and she smiled. Aside from a few bits and bobs, there was only one thing still missing from the room, she thought as she tidied up the packaging and prepared to put it in the trash—that special baby smell and the infant who'd bring it. He'd be there all too soon, and then her work would be done. The thought was both reassuring and a little saddening at the same time.

It was the hardest part of her job, reaching the end of a contract. Knowing a new family was on the precipice of a shared journey that she'd never experience for herself. It was a feeling she'd become used to but that never made it hurt any less.

She picked up the pacifiers and airtight containers she'd bought for storing them in and took them downstairs to be sterilized. As she neared the bottom of the stairs she heard a door down the corridor to her left close.

"You're all finished?" Ronin asked as he strolled down the hall toward her.

"I just need to sterilize these and then I'm all yours."

"I like the sound of that," he answered. "And I hope you'll like the sound of what I've got planned for you."

"I'm intrigued," Ali admitted with a grin. "Any hints?"

"Be patient and you'll find out," Ronin answered with an enigmatic smile.

He took her through to the kitchen, where she extracted the sterilizing equipment from the bottom of a cupboard.

"Here," Ali said, gesturing to the items she'd collated on the benchtop. "I'll instruct, you do."

"Me? Won't the nannies be doing all that?" he asked, taking the pacifiers from her and staring at them as if they were something to be dissected and studied.

"Absolutely. But you should still know what to do, even if you have the nannies here around the clock. I think you should still be hands-on."

"My sister trusted me enough to put her son in my care, so I guess I owe it to her."

Together they went through the steps outlined on the packaging. They were just finishing up when Ali heard a beating rotor noise, which got louder and louder and then tapered away, like a helicopter being shut down.

"There's that clue you wanted," Ronin commented. "Hungry?"

"You're taking me to lunch in a helicopter?"

"Ever been in one before?"

Ali shook her head. She'd always wanted to ride in one, but the tour flights offered in the city were so expensive.

"Then you're in for a treat."

Ali got her things together quickly and followed Ronin out the big sliding glass doors that led out through the kitchen and family room. Sure enough, about fifty meters from the house sat a gleaming black helicopter with the words REM Consulting emblazoned in gold on its tail.

"This is *yours*?" she asked incredulously.

"Well, it's my company's, to be more precise. While we contract overseas a great deal, about forty percent of our work is here in New Zealand. Sometimes we need to get to places that commercial flights and hired cars can't get to quickly or easily."

Ali tried not to look overawed as Ronin introduced her to the pilot and then handed her up into the cabin, but she had a feeling she failed miserably. There, he showed her how to buckle her seat belt and adjust her headset before he climbed in next to her. Her stomach gave a delighted flip as the pilot completed preflight checks and the machine lifted into the sky. She'd already thought the view from Ronin's house toward the harbor was without par, but this bird's-eye view was truly amazing.

The rain from earlier in the morning had cleared and the sun shone on the rippled surface of the sea as they flew toward Waiheke Island. In far too short a time, they descended outside what looked like a vineyard with a

restaurant. Ronin showed her into the restaurant building, where a cheery fire burned in a fireplace in one
wall. This early in autumn it wasn't strictly necessary,
but it lent a delightful ambience to the dining room.

She couldn't remember ever having anyone pay her
quite as much attention as Ronin did. She and Richard
had known each other so long and had been so comfortable together they'd lost touch with the little things that
made a marriage sparkle like new again. It scared her
that she was enjoying herself so much and that Ronin
could make her feel so special and, with each lingering glance, wanted. She'd have to be made of stone not
to respond.

"See anything you like?" he asked as they perused
their menus.

Oh, she saw something she liked, all right. And it had
nothing to do with the menu in her hand. It was something more like forbidden fruit. A delight, once tasted,
that remained forever on your tongue, inciting a crav-
ing that was almost too hard to resist. *Almost.*

Ali dragged her gaze away from the man seated
across the table and scanned the menu again.

"It's too hard to choose," she said on a huff of air.
"There's so much on here that I love. Why don't you
select something for me? I promise you, you can't go
wrong."

"Whatever the lady wants," he replied, lifting his
gaze to mesh with hers briefly.

Ali felt her whole body bloom under his attention,
her senses coming to life like a neglected garden after a
drenching rain. His unrelenting interest in her was both
thrilling and terrifying in equal proportion. She wanted
to take a step back, to create a sense of safety and space

between them—a distance between right now and that night in Hawaii. But could she hold out against his allure? More importantly, did she really want to?

Six

Ronin savored the rising tide of desire that ebbed and flowed through his veins as he watched Ali enjoy the food he'd chosen for her. He'd always considered it chauvinistic to order for a woman, but when Ali had surrendered the choice to him, he'd felt a sense of honor that she'd entrusted him with the job.

Her tongue swept her upper lip as she finished the last of the ripe camembert from the cheeseboard and crackers he'd selected as their dessert. He remembered, all too well, how that tongue had felt on his body, and he wanted to experience it again.

Softly, softly, he reminded himself. There was a wounded fragility about her that he'd discerned beneath the capable businesswoman who'd taken over the nursery at the house. He had a feeling it wouldn't take much to frighten her away, and that was very definitely the last thing he wanted to do.

"Good?" he asked, as she took a sip of the Pinot Gris he'd chosen to go with their meal and sighed.

"Perfect. Everything is perfect."

"I aim to please," he said lowly, letting her see in his eyes that he meant to please her in *all* things.

To his delight a flush of color highlighted her cheeks and she dropped her gaze, her dark lashes sweeping down to hide the expression in her eyes. But he could see the sudden flutter of her pulse at the base of the pale column of her throat. He ached to kiss her there again. Soon, he promised himself. Soon.

The other day she'd mentioned a time when she'd been at a crossroads in her life. The engineer in him wanted to pick what she'd said apart, to understand exactly what had happened to give her that air of fragility he saw when her guard was down. It was only after you pulled something apart and put it back together that you could fully understand a problem and begin to solve it.

But, while fixing problems was something he was very good at, he sensed she'd throw her barriers back up again if he attempted to pick her pain and her troubles apart. No, he had to go slowly, to let her come to him in her own time. Still, he considered as her eyes lifted to his again and he saw the warmth in them reflecting back at him, there was no harm in stepping up the pace just a little.

After lunch the helicopter returned to fly them back to the house. Before they did, Ronin asked his pilot to take them on a low-flying scenic journey of the inner harbor and its islands. Ali's excitement and pleasure in the flight was palpable, and he found himself smiling in response as she exclaimed over yet another feature she recognized beneath them.

At the house, after they'd disembarked from the

chopper and gone back inside, she turned to give him a beatific smile.

"That was, without doubt, the best lunch of my life," she gushed. "It was amazing, Ronin."

"I'm glad you enjoyed it. I did, too."

"I really don't know how to thank you properly."

He took a step closer to her, his hands reaching for her waist. "I do," he said firmly, and pulled her toward him.

Her lips were soft and lush as he claimed them, and he was hard-pressed to control the urge to take them fiercely, to plunder their sweetness. He'd meant to let her come to him of her own volition, and he'd taken a risk doing this, but a surge of exaltation washed through him as her lips parted against his and her tongue slid between his lips.

Her kiss was so giving, its effect so instantaneous, that a tremor of need shuddered through him. A groan escaped his mouth as her form molded to his, as she fitted herself against him, her softness absorbing all of him that was hard and aching. Fire lit in his groin, sending fingers of heat to scorch through his body and igniting a powerful passion. One that clouded rational behavior and grew stronger and more demanding every second they touched.

Ali's hands rose to his head, her fingers threading through his short hair and holding him close as their tongues met and retreated, only to meet again. He was starving for her, all of her. The pulse in his body made him harden even more as desire overcame thought and reason, making its demands clear. He pressed his hips against hers, groaning again as his erection nudged her pelvis.

Ali pulled her head away, her breath coming in rapid

gasps, her hands falling to his wrists where she gently forced him to let her go.

"Ronin, I—" she started.

He pressed a short kiss to her mouth, fighting the need to make it more persuasive. He knew he could. But that didn't mean she'd welcome it, or him—especially when she'd been the first to disengage from their embrace.

"Don't," he said gruffly. "No need for an explanation. It's okay."

They were difficult words to enunciate when every cell, every nerve, in his body clamored for their contact to resume. For each wet kiss, for each fervent touch, to progress to its natural conclusion. Ronin forced his recalcitrant libido back under control.

Ali dipped her head. "I'm sorry." The words were so quiet he wasn't even sure he'd heard right. "I'd better go."

"Don't be sorry. I'm not. You're a beautiful woman, Ali Carter—inside and out. I want to know you better, and I'm prepared to wait if that's what it takes."

How long he could continue to wait might be an issue, he thought as his flesh strained against the confines of his briefs. But then again, that's what punishing workouts at midnight in his home gym and icy cold showers were for, right?

She lifted her face and looked at him. "Where are we going with this, Ronin?"

He'd have thought that was obvious. "I'd like to think we're getting to know one another."

"You're my client."

"And I'd like to be more." *Much more.*

She shook her head. "No. Look, what I said before about Hawaii, about that not being me? I meant it. I'm not normally that person. That's not to say that I regret it—what we did together was, well, great. But that's all it was. A holiday fling. A one-off. I'm not in the market for anything else, Ronin. I've been hurt before. Badly hurt. I will not put myself through that again."

A primitive roar surged within him. He wanted to protect her, to wipe the slate clean of her past hurts, past regrets. He wanted to make her world right. But she had to let him. The ultimate control lay within her.

"I don't plan to hurt you, Ali. Anything, everything, but that."

She shook her head. "There are things about me you don't know. I've been married before, for starters."

"And you aren't now, which makes getting to know you a great deal simpler, wouldn't you say?"

She shook her head. "Don't joke about this, Ronin. It's not open to discussion."

"I'm sorry. I know firsthand how you feel about infidelity, and if it's any consolation, I feel the same way. But I'm not prepared to give up on you, Ali Carter. We first met by accident. We were lucky enough to meet again. Some might call it fate, but I don't believe in that. What I do believe in is what I know, what I can substantiate—that we potentially have something I've never had with anyone before. Give us a chance."

He studied her carefully. Her lips, still glistening with moisture, were softly swollen from his kiss. Her skin was flushed, her breathing shallow. A pulse leapt at the base of her throat. But her eyes made him draw in a breath and take a moment. While her body showed all the signs of arousal, her eyes still held shadows. Who was it, he thought, who had done such a number on her? Who had hurt her so badly that she could do what he was unable to and put mental strength before physical demand when it came to their fiery attraction?

She shook her head again, more emphatically this time. "Please respect me on this. Let's keep our relationship purely business. If you don't agree, I don't think I can continue to work for you."

He sighed and shoved his hands in his trouser pockets. "Okay. Business." *For now,* he added silently.

Ali had double-checked the supplies in the kitchen and triple-checked the nursery. Everything was perfect for the baby's homecoming today. The past few days since their lunch together had been…well, difficult. While Ronin hadn't put any pressure on her, she could still feel the hunger that rolled off him in waves every time they were together. A hunger that she had to admit she shared. Even though he'd spent more time at his office in the city, they'd still crossed paths a few times, and each time she'd felt every cell in her body go on alert. She didn't know what was worse. Anticipating their meetings or arriving at the house—like she had today—and finding he wasn't there.

At least her role was coming to an end. It was finally okay for the baby to come home, so Ronin had organized to collect his nephew, together with his parents, and bring them all back to his house this afternoon. For the first week the baby was home, Ronin and parents would care for him, and from next week, the rotation of nannies would begin. It had been a big job to pull together in the time they'd had, but it was done—and done to perfection, Ali thought as she swiped an imaginary speck of dust from the top rail of the baby's crib.

He wouldn't be sleeping there any time soon, though, she thought with a smile. While he was still small he'd be in the adorable bassinet she'd found online and had express-shipped here two days ago.

She hated to admit it, but this job had become a complete labor of love. She'd always managed to maintain a degree of separation during nursery fit outs before. It had been something she'd learned to do out of necessity. It was one thing to pour all your love and expectations for a child into your work—quite another when you got too invested and forgot that the children you worked to care for would never be your own. No, emotional distance was key. But with this job it had been different.

Maybe it was because of the circumstances of this infant's birth, or maybe it had more to do with the man who'd become the child's guardian. Either way, Ali had poured her heart into every last detail. The room was perfect. She took one last glance and then turned to put it, and Ronin Marshall, behind her.

She was at the top of the main stairs when she heard a car pull up outside. How had someone gotten through the main gates? She wasn't expecting any deliveries, and to spare herself the turmoil, she had planned to be gone before Ronin and his parents returned with the baby. So who could it be?

A car door closed, and, after a pause, another. She heard footsteps coming into the front portico. A few seconds later, the door opened to reveal an older, slightly shorter version of Ronin, carrying an infant car seat.

His face was gray and drawn, his faded blue eyes filled with anxiety.

"Oh, thank God you're here!" he said with vehement relief.

"Mr. Marshall?"

"Yes," he answered. "My wife, she collapsed at the hospital as we were leaving with the baby—they've taken her into the ER. I have to get back to her, but someone needs to care for my grandson, here."

"Ronin was called to fly out urgently just as we arrived at the hospital. He said he'd ring you and see if you could bring the start date forward for the nannies. That's what you're waiting here for, isn't it? For the nanny to arrive? Please say that's so."

Ronin had called her? Ali felt a clutch in her chest. She'd left her phone in her bag at the bottom of the stairs when she'd arrived. Being upstairs, she wouldn't have heard it ring. The house phone had sounded a few times, but with it not being her home she'd left it unanswered. None of that mattered right now, though, as Ronin's father appeared increasingly distraught.

"Don't worry, Mr. Marshall, I'll take care of things."

He thrust the baby carrier toward her.

"Thank you. I'd stay, but I really must get back. I just knew this would all be too much for Delia. We'd just gotten to the car when she collapsed. Before they took her into ER she made me promise I'd bring our grandson out here, to his new home. And anyway, I couldn't wait around the ER with him."

"I understand," Ali said soothingly, even though inside her nerves were jumping like water droplets on a hot skillet. "He'll be fine with me for now. You take care on the trip back to town, okay?"

He looked at her a moment, his eyes stricken. "I will. Thank you. I can see why Ronin speaks so highly of you, and why he was so certain you'd have things under control."

He did? A bloom of warmth filled her heart. Ali adjusted the weight of the car seat in her arms and looked down at the tiny life cocooned in there. Her heart flipped over. She'd wanted to avoid this—potentially falling in love with the tiny tot—but one glance and she was done for. Only a couple of weeks old and he'd already lost so much. She ached to cuddle him close and make him feel loved.

"I will take good care of him," she promised, her voice infused with all the assurance she was capable of.

"I'll be off then." He was already halfway down the front stairs when he realized he still had a bag filled with baby supplies on his shoulder. "I'd better leave this with you, too. It's some formula and clothes and other things that Delia put together for his homecoming, as well as the release notes from the hospital."

"Thank you. If you could leave it just inside I'll grab it once I've settled him in his bassinet."

Ronin's father's gaze lingered on his grandson. "Delia so wanted to be here when he came home. When Ronin had to leave us at the hospital and go straight out to the airport she was adamant that we carry on as planned. She didn't want the baby in the hospital a moment longer than he needed to be. Ronin doesn't even know his mother's ill. I hope she'll be okay." His voice broke on the words. "She's got to be."

"Mr. Marshall." Ali placed one hand on his trembling arm. "Your wife is in the best place possible. Don't you worry about a thing here. I have it all under control, okay? You go and be where you're most needed. Call the house if you want to check on us, or if you want to let me know how Mrs. Marshall is doing."

"I will," he said, and with a half-hearted attempt at a wave he walked swiftly toward his car.

It was only once he'd driven away that Ali realized that no one had told her the baby's name. Not once in the past week and a half with Ronin had he mentioned it, and she'd been too startled to find Ronin's father on the front steps just now to even think of asking him. What was she supposed to call him? Baby X? *Think,* she urged her sluggish brain. The solution presented itself almost immediately. Of course, his name would be on the release notes tucked in the diaper bag.

Ali closed the front door and looked again at the sleeping child. The enormity of what she'd just agreed to do settled over her like a lead cloak as anxiety coiled like a snake in the pit of her belly. It would only be for a few hours, max, she assured herself as she began to ascend the stairs. As soon as baby was settled, she'd be on the phone to the nanny service to see who would be able to start early.

Her stomach did a nervous flip as the infant squirmed a little—his tiny face screwing up, his mouth twisting—before, to her great relief, he settled again. What would she do if he cried? The logical side of her brain kicked into action. It wasn't difficult, she tried to assure herself. She knew the basics. Besides, if he was still at risk, they wouldn't have released him from the hospital today. She'd do whatever needed doing. She'd check his diaper, she'd feed him if he needed feeding, and if none of that worked, well, she'd just hold him.

Hold him. The thought in itself shouldn't have made her tremble with anxiety. She'd handled babies before. Her three older sisters had seven kids between them and Ali had been hands-on at every stage of her nieces' and nephews' lives. *This shouldn't be any different,* she assured herself as she carried the car seat upstairs to the nursery. *This shouldn't be any different at all.*

And yet, when it came to unbuckling the belt that secured him, she was all thumbs.

"This is ridiculous," she muttered to herself. "Get your act together."

Unsnapping the clip, she eased the straps away from the baby's tiny body and scooped her hands beneath him, taking extra care to support his head. He was so small, so light—like a doll almost. And yet he was strong and tenacious, as well. He'd fought through a tough delivery and against breathing difficulties to be well enough to get released from hospital. There was no need to be unduly concerned about him. All she needed to do until help arrived was provide him with a safe place to sleep and food to eat. She could do that.

Ali held his tiny body against her chest as she pulled back the cover on the bassinet. He nestled against her automatically, as if seeking that nurturing care that only a cuddle could bring. It was with great reluctance that she laid him on the pristine white sheet that covered the mattress. His little arms flung out as she released him, startling him awake. She looked for the first time into his blue eyes.

"There, there," she soothed, rubbing his chest until his eyes slid closed again.

Before she pulled the coverlet up, she saw the hospital ID tag that remained on his ankle. His name was right there. Although the surname had become obscured, his first name stood out clearly—Joshua. Tears stung her eyes and she drew in a deep breath to combat the painful wrench that pulled at her from deep inside. Joshua was the name she and Richard had chosen for their first-born child, if he were to be a boy. Except their firstborn child had never even been conceived.

It shouldn't hurt this much, she told herself. Lots of little boys the world over were called Joshua. It was a lovely name, a great name—that's why she and her ex had chosen it themselves. But somehow, knowing this poor motherless child was named Joshua was her undoing.

First one tear, then another, slid down her face. She swallowed a gulp of grief for the baby boy she'd never have and forced herself to tuck Joshua into his bassinet, and then she left the room. Outside she leaned against the wall until she could get her emotions under control. This was too hard, too much. She needed to contact the agency and get the appropriate help so she could get out of here right now. She cursed the fact she hadn't received any of Ronin's calls and fervently wished she could speak to him right now, but if he was in the air already and on his way to Vietnam it would be hours before he'd land. Besides, even if she reached him, what would she say? That she didn't want to care for his nephew because the baby reminded her of all she couldn't have?

Instead she straightened slowly from the wall, squared her shoulders and silently stepped back into the nursery to check on Joshua. He was still exactly as she'd left him. She needlessly adjusted his covers then activated the baby monitor and left to go downstairs. In the kitchen she activated the monitor's partner unit and then she delved into her handbag for her phone. Three missed calls and one new message. She listened to the message—it was from Ronin, as she'd expected.

His warm, deep voice filled her ear, and she told herself it was ridiculous to feel a sense of relief at his tone. There was nothing he could do for her right now. He'd left on business secure in the knowledge that his nephew was being cared for—now it was up to her to make sure that happened. After explaining how long he'd probably be away and asking her to organize at least one of the

nannies to start earlier to help his parents, he closed off
with, "I'll call you as soon as I land in Hanoi."

Well, she had to be satisfied with that. There was
nothing else she could do for now except leave a message on his phone and, given what the family had been
through already, to assure him that she had everything
under control. She said nothing of his mother's urgent admission to hospital. It wouldn't be fair to im-
part that kind of news in a message. He needed to hear
that person-to-person. With a deep sigh, she scrolled
through her contacts for the nanny service she'd used
and pressed Call.

Sixty minutes of frustration later, Ali was forced to
admit defeat. Ronin's initial brief on what he wanted in
a nanny had been explicit. He wanted people with neo-
natal care experience and a proven track record as a private nanny in the bargain. He already had the four best
candidates for the position lined up to work in rotating
twelve-hour shifts, four days on, four days off—starting
next week. Not a single one could start any earlier and,
given their expertise and the demand for their skills, Ali
wasn't all that surprised. And the backup candidates
she'd considered had all accepted other placements.

Even calls to a private nursing agency had proven
fruitless, and she already knew the other agencies she'd
used from time to time currently had no one suitable
and available on their books.

A squawk over the monitor had her heart pounding.
Joshua was waking. He'd need attention, and there was
no one else here but her to give it to him. She flew up the
stairs and into the nursery, where his reedy cry built up
in tempo. She scooped him up into her arms and began
to rock from side to side, humming a tuneless sound in
an attempt to soothe him.

Yes, she'd assured Ronin's dad that the baby would be all right and that she'd look after things, but that was when she'd thought she'd be able to hand over the responsibility to someone who was far more experienced and capable with an infant than she was herself. She wasn't in any way as qualified as the nannies Ronin had selected to care for this poor mother- and fatherless babe. *But right here, right now?* It was she who was left holding the baby.

Literally.

Seven

Ronin disembarked from the plane and strode through the airport, getting through customs and immigration with the weary acceptance of a frequent long-distance traveler. It had never bothered him before, but after four frustratingly endless days it seemed to him that this game was most definitely for someone else. Someone, perhaps, who had less responsibility here at home.

He'd already called his dad the moment phone use had been permitted after landing. Thankfully his mother was steadily improving. She was as comfortable as could be expected after coronary bypass surgery, and his dad hoped she'd be home within the next couple of days.

Guilt for leaving town in the first place had battered him during the entire trip, especially once he'd belatedly received the news about his mother's condition. When his father called, Ronin had been stuck in Hanoi—bound by the strictures of the contract he'd agreed to with his client and bound to solve the issues that had arisen, as swiftly as possible. Besides, as his father had pointed out to him, his mother was receiving excellent care and making steady progress with her recovery. Him being there, or not, would make no difference at this stage.

And then there was Ali. She'd been singlehandedly taking care of Joshua for them. A role that was way above and beyond anything he could have anticipated or expected. He'd heard the weariness in her voice when he'd managed to speak with her before boarding in Hanoi more than seventeen hours ago. She'd assured him that Joshua was fine, and that a home care nurse had visited in a follow-up from the hospital, but there'd been a note of strain in her voice that worried him.

His dad had been out to the house a couple of times to help where he could, and he'd assured Ronin that Ali was coping well. Still, nothing would convince him that everything was all right until he could see it for himself.

The drive home from the airport took forever, but Ronin felt himself relaxing in increments as he headed out of the built-up zones and toward Whitford. He called Ali from the car when he was about twenty minutes from the house.

"Hello, Marshall residence," her voice replied, so very correctly.

"It's me," he said with a smile. "Is there anything you need me to pick up on the way through?"

As much as he didn't want to stop en route, he realized she'd been pretty much housebound in a place that wasn't her own home from the day he'd left.

"No, it's okay. Deb brought some things out to me and I've had groceries delivered."

Just come home. The message wasn't spoken, but it was there in the underlying tone of her voice. A tone that said, while she was coping, she really wasn't happy about the situation at all.

"Okay, I'll be there soon."

"I'll see you then."

He disconnected, but not before he heard her faint sigh over the car speakers. He thought again about the mammoth undertaking she'd accepted when she'd agreed to stay on at the house with his nephew. He had only intended her responsibilities to last a couple of hours, and yet they had stretched out into four, nearly five, days. He owed her—big time. He pressed his foot down a little more firmly on the accelerator, more eager than ever to cover the final miles to his home.

He'd always prided himself on his personal attention to a job and yet, in this most important role he'd ever agreed to take on, he'd been horribly remiss. Something had to change, and it needed to change right now. He'd also always prided himself on succession planning at work, on training up his second and third in charge to be able to step into the breach when necessary. But what good was succession planning if you didn't pass on responsibility to someone else when you needed to? When he'd agreed to take on the responsibility of his nephew's guardianship he hadn't thought beyond the immediate issues, but it was clear now that he hadn't considered every contingency. Things were going to be very different from now on. It would be an adjustment, but he'd figure out how to make it work—he was good at that.

Ali was in the front entrance as he drove his car up the drive. He felt that familiar sense of heat and desire pulling at him the moment he identified her standing there. Dressed in form-fitting jeans and a long-sleeved

T-shirt, she was certainly turned out more casually than he'd become used to seeing her, although she was no less attractive for it. Not even bothering to put his car in the garage, he parked and got out, walking straight over to her. His cases—hell, everything else—could wait.

He shortened the distance between them with long strides, fighting the urge to pull her into his arms the moment she was within reach. She was paler than usual, her eyes were more shadowed and her high cheekbones appeared more prominent. Had she lost weight?

"Ali, I can't begin to thank you—" he started.

"There's no need for thanks. Joshie needed someone to care for him and I was here. That's all there is to it."

Despite her reassurance, he could hear the note of strain in her voice. Clearly it hadn't been easy. Was there something wrong with the baby? Had he been unwell?

"Joshua? How is he?"

"He's doing great. I think the home care nurse was a bit surprised to find me caring for him, but I seem to have passed with full marks."

"I wouldn't have expected you to do anything less," he said, forcing a smile to his lips. If there was one thing among the many things he'd noticed about Alison Carter, it was that she was competent and capable. "Is he upstairs?"

They headed through the front door, and then Ronin turned toward the staircase.

"No, I have him downstairs. I ordered a second bassinet for down here so I could keep working while I watched him. I hope you don't mind, but I commandeered the kitchen dining table as a makeshift office and popped Joshua in the living room next door during the day."

A pang of guilt struck him. He'd been so absorbed

in doing what was right for his own business that he'd barely given any consideration to hers. The debt he owed her kept mounting.

"Of course I don't mind. I'm deeply grateful to you for stepping in when my family needed you most." *When I needed you most,* he added silently.

"I'm glad I could help."

She smiled, but it didn't quite reach her eyes. Eyes that were underscored by the purplish bruises of weariness and strain. He was sorely tempted to reach out and touch her, as if he could gently wipe away those traces of darkness. But his touch couldn't magically heal whatever hurt she carried with her—if she'd even accept his touch in the first place, he growled silently as he curled his hand into a fist in his pocket.

"It's been tough?" he asked.

Her lips pulled into a tight smile. "A little," she admitted. "But he's a beautiful baby. In fact I think he's quite stolen my heart."

"Yeah, he seems to have that effect on people. I've been looking forward to seeing him again."

A cry from inside the house made them both turn their heads.

Ali gave a short laugh. "And it sounds like he's heard your arrival and wants to see you, too."

They went through from the foyer and down the hall toward the family room as the baby's cries became more insistent. Ronin hesitated when he saw the bassinet over by the French doors.

"He's ready for a feed. Would you like to do it?" she asked.

"Sure," he said, still a little unsure about the precious bundle squirming and squalling in his bassinet.

Ali looked up at him. "You didn't feed him in the hospital?"

Ronin shook his head. "Mum did that, whenever our hospital visits coincided with mealtimes. Guess I've gotta learn sometime. Should I wash my hands first?"

Ali pointed over to the kitchen sink, where she'd obviously put a bottle of antiseptic hand wash. "You can do it there while I change his diaper."

She moved over to the baby and, seemingly unaffected by his cries, lifted him from his bassinet onto a folding change table she'd set up nearby. She was just fastening the sides on Joshua's clean diaper when he returned.

"I guess I'd better get some experience in that too, huh?" he said dubiously.

Ali cracked a smile. "You certainly will, but I've let you off the hook with this one."

"Thanks. So, feeding him. Do I sit down?"

"I usually sit over there," Ali said, gesturing to an easy chair set in the corner by the doors.

"Come on," Ali urged him. "Pick him up while I warm his bottle."

Pick him up? Ronin forced his feet in the direction of the change table, but he came to an abrupt halt when he saw the demanding red face above the blue-and-white striped onesie that encased his nephew.

"Don't be frightened," Ali said softly. "You handled him before at the hospital, right?"

"Kind of," Ronin said, suddenly feeling underprepared, a sensation he had never enjoyed. He'd thought he was ready for this, but it seemed that it was one thing to have the nurses lay Joshua in his arms, and quite another to pick him up himself.

"Here," Ali said, leaning over the change table and

deftly scooping the squalling infant up. She handed him to Ronin. "Hold him against you, like this." She guided one of his hands to the back of Joshua's head and the other to his bottom. "There. You're a natural."

Her words were reassuring, especially with Joshua's cries suddenly ceasing and his little face burrowing against the fine cotton of Ronin's shirtfront. Ali moved away from him to the kitchen, where she washed her hands, efficiently warmed some formula and then brought the small bottle over to Ronin.

"He can still be a bit fussy over the bottle, but just persevere and he'll get the message."

Fussy? What did she mean by that? Didn't babies just drink? He soon found out that just because Joshua was hungry, it didn't mean he was entirely happy to actually have to work at being fed.

"He's a bit of a rascal, but he's better now than he has been," Ali said from her vantage point beside him.

There was a wealth of things unsaid in her words. Again Ronin felt that pang of guilt over the burden he had left her to shoulder alone. He got a solid hint of what she meant as the baby took his own good time to latch on to the bottle. He found himself caught by Joshua's stare as he finally drank. He'd had nothing to do with babies before Joshie's birth. It had all seemed to be a great idea when CeeCee and R.J. had talked about his duties as uncle, but the reality of now being wholly responsible for this tiny life came crashing down onto him like a tidal wave.

It all rested on his shoulders now. Everything. Caring for this little person wasn't something he could chart on a spreadsheet. He couldn't draw up a diagram for satisfying all the baby's needs, nor could he calculate every possible risk. He would have to bear the load alone, a situation his usual methods would do nothing to resolve. Caring for Joshua would be a trial by fire—for both of them. It was pretty daunting.

He looked up from the little person in his arms to see Ali moving about the family room, gathering up her things and putting away her papers and the laptop computer she'd set up on the table.

"What are you doing?" he asked.

"Packing up and getting ready to go home."

"Why?"

"Because you're back now, that's why."

An unfamiliar sensation rippled through him. She was leaving him? With the baby? Alone?

"There's no need for you to rush off."

She paused in the middle of sliding her laptop into a vibrant pink leather case. "I thought you'd prefer to have some time alone with Joshua. Get to know one another a little better."

"Ali, I haven't the slightest idea what to do with this baby. Please stay. At least until the nannies start on Monday. I'll make it worth your while." He added the last as a final incentive in the hope it might sway her.

Ali felt her chest constrict. He had no idea what he was asking her to do. Over the past few days she'd been forced to face so many of her hopes and dreams that had always been tied up in having a baby of her own to love and care for. She'd thought she'd moved past those dreams when she learned they could never come true, but the longing was still there. It had been distressing to attempt to hold herself aloof from Joshua, and in the end, and to what she suspected would be her eternal cost, she'd crumbled, giving him her heart despite her best intentions to protect herself. She already fiercely loved this baby, who she'd known from the start she wouldn't be able to keep.

She'd looked forward to Ronin's return so she could leave—for selfish reasons, she admitted. Her job was done, she affirmed quietly, and now it was time to go. She needed to distance herself from them both. She could never be part of their family, and it was better to abandon the illusion now before she risked being hurt even more.

It had crucified her when her own husband, a man she'd loved since she was sixteen years old, fell out of love with her when they found she was the reason they couldn't have a baby of their own. Yes, they'd built the foundation of their future on their plans to have a family, and yes, it had been her fault that they couldn't have children of their own. But she had thought he loved *her* more than he loved his plans for their picture-perfect life together. She'd been wrong.

Himself a late surprise to older parents, as well as an only child, Richard had always joked about creating their own dynasty. When she'd suggested adoption he'd been strangely reluctant. When he'd come home one day and said he was leaving her to be with someone else, that he *loved* that someone else, it had shocked her to her core. She had still loved him, still wanted to make their marriage work. Thousands—hundreds of thousands—of couples were childless, either by choice or chance, and still lived long and happy lives together.

But he hadn't been prepared to give up his chance to have a family. It had devastated her. She wouldn't, no, *couldn't* put herself in the path of that freight train again. It had been hard enough to fight out of the misery and eventually put herself back together after Richard had left her. She doubted she'd find the strength to do it again.

That made it all the more important to protect herself now. To shore up the walls she needed around her heart before she lost herself to Ronin and Joshua completely.

Ronin sat there, holding the baby and looking at her. Obviously expecting an answer.

"It's not about the money," she said.

He kept looking at her with an expression in his eyes that she struggled to define. It was almost a challenge and yet there was a plea reflected there as well. Ali struggled for the right words to turn him down.

"Look," she sighed, "I can't work as effectively from here as I do in my office, and I really can't leave Deb managing all on her own for the rest of this week. It's not fair to her or to the rest of Best for Baby's clientele. I've already spent far too much time away from my office."

"I understand," he said. "But if I could arrange some assistance for Deb in the office, and take on some of Joshua's care myself to free you up a bit more during the day to work as you have been doing, would you reconsider?"

She watched him with the baby and realized that the bottle was now empty, and Joshua was still sucking furiously at it.

"You'll have to take the bottle from his mouth. He's just sucking air now."

Ronin tried to pull the bottle from the baby's mouth, but now Joshua was latched on he wasn't letting go. Ronin cast her a helpless look.

"Here," she said, moving to his side. "Slide the tip of your little finger into the corner of his mouth to break the suction. Then you'll need to burp him."

She took the bottle from Ronin. Turning to grab a soft towel from the stack folded on the table beside the chair, she lay it on his shoulder.

"Now, lift him to your shoulder and rub his back. He's okay with a firm touch. It'll help him bring up the wind."

Ronin did everything she said, and his expression when Joshua belched was a picture. Despite her desire to flee this man and child and the way they reminded her of all of her deficiencies, she still felt compelled to do as he asked—to stay.

"You really have no idea, do you?" she asked, her voice soft.

"None whatsoever. Mum was going to be in charge of helping me until the nannies started, but..." He shrugged helplessly, jiggling his tiny charge on his shoulder. The baby let out another burp.

Ali was torn. Ronin hadn't asked for this responsibility to land in his lap. All his plans had gone awry when his mother had collapsed. Even Neil, his father, had been fingers and thumbs with the baby the few times he'd come out to give Ali a hand.

This was going to destroy her, she just knew it. Every day she would fall more deeply in love with the baby, and, she recognized, very likely with Ronin, too—no matter how hard she fought it. She'd be setting herself up for hurt and failure when the time inevitably came to leave them behind—two things she'd already had more than her fair share of.

Logically, she knew, her job here was done, and she needed to run and run fast to avoid the pain that surely lingered on the horizon. She didn't want to fall in love again. It hurt too much. But, against her better judgment, the words formed in her mouth.

"Fine. I'll stay."

Eight

Ronin rose with the baby in his arms and came toward her. Her first instinct was to fend them off. This was not what she'd anticipated when she'd taken on this job with him—not by any means.

She didn't want to think about how he was everything she'd ever wanted in a man. Strong and capable. The kind of guy who could take charge in any situation and make things happen. An amazing lover.

No! She slammed the door on that thought. That was a line she couldn't afford to cross again. If she did, she might as well just throw herself on a railroad track and wait for the next train. The effect would be the same.

And he came complete with a precious, adorable baby who already had her wrapped around his tiny little fingers. Again her heart tugged hard, but she took a step back, her action making Ronin halt in his tracks. A wary expression passed across his face.

"Thank you, Ali. I appreciate your staying. And I mean it about making it worth your while. I'll get Maeve, my P.A., to send someone from our office to help Deb out. I assume she'll need someone who can answer calls, take messages and do a bit of filing. Take care of the grunt work while she attends to the more important things?"

Ali grasped hold of his offer and went with it. "Yes, that would be fine. It'll only be for a couple of days, after all."

"I think I know just the person. She's not an office junior—far from it. In fact she's probably one of our most senior staff members, in terms of age and office experience. She'll be an excellent asset in assisting Deb."

"She sounds perfect," Ali replied woodenly.

And it should be great, except it meant she had no excuse to leave Ronin's home. Deb had already been to her apartment and packed enough clothing for her when Ronin had first gone overseas. She could claim she needed to run by her apartment and pick up some more things, but it would just be an excuse to give herself a little time away. She'd made the commitment to stay, and now she had to stick to it.

She looked at the man and the child only a meter in front of her and felt a physical ache deep inside her chest. It would be all too easy to just let go of that hard-earned control. To allow herself to follow where her instincts were trying so hard to lead. But it wouldn't end well. She might be able to keep them for a little while, but it wouldn't last for long. She was damaged goods. Richard had made that patently clear.

"Can I give you Joshua so I can call Maeve right away?"

Ali cast an eye over the baby, who appeared to have dozed off in his uncle's arms.

"Actually, now would be a good time to learn how to swaddle him and put him back down in his bassinet."

"Swaddle him? Sounds difficult."

She'd thought the same when she'd discovered Joshua would keep startling and waking himself in the night. Exhausted after two nights and two very full days of unsettled baby, she'd eventually called her mother for a suggestion on what to do. Her mum had described the way she'd wrapped and put her own babies to sleep. She'd ended with, "Don't you remember? Each of your sisters did the same with theirs, too."

She did remember and had kicked herself for not thinking of it. Her first attempts had been abysmal, but by the end of her third day she'd had it down pat.

"Bring him over here," she said to Ronin, who followed her to the bassinet. "I've used squares of muslin because they're what my sisters used and because his bed covers are warm enough and I don't want him to get overheated. I'll order some fitted wraps, though. They're a lot simpler to use."

She put down the fabric and told Ronin to put Joshua in the middle. Then she folded the bottom flap up and the edges over, wrapping him until he was secure.

"See?" she said. "It's quite straightforward."

"You're a natural," Ronin replied. "Have you never thought about having a child of your own?"

Ali closed her eyes briefly and swallowed. *Only every single day of my life until about five years ago,* she thought to herself. Ignoring his question, she unwrapped the baby and stepped back from the bassinet.

"It'll come easily to you, too, once you get in a bit of practice. There, you have a go," she encouraged.

He did as she had demonstrated. It wasn't perfect, but it was a whole lot better than her first attempts.

"Looks like you're a natural yourself," she said with a forced smile. "Now leave him on his back and tuck his covers around him. He'll be okay for hopefully the next couple of hours."

"That's it? That's all he does? Eat and sleep?"

"And poop, but that's a lesson for another time." Her smile was more relaxed this time.

"Shouldn't he be upstairs in his nursery, where it's quiet?"

"It's probably a good idea for him to learn to sleep in any environment. You're not always going to be able to ensure perfect sleeping conditions for him while you're out or visiting your parents."

"Good point," Ronin said, eyeing the wee bundle in the white cane bassinet. "I had no idea it would be like this. The responsibility, I mean. How can I be sure that I'm going to make the right decisions for him?"

His honesty struck a chord with her. On a smaller scale she'd felt like that from the moment she'd realized she was solely responsible for the baby's care until Ronin's return. "You just have to trust yourself. The way your sister and her husband trusted you when they named you Joshie's guardian."

And, she realized, she had to trust herself, too. Trust herself not to let her guard down and open her heart any further to the man and the child before her.

Ronin woke with a start as the sound of Joshua's cry disturbed his slumber—again. For a second he was disoriented, the night-shaded surrounding of his master bedroom momentarily unfamiliar to him. But then it all came crashing back, and he got to his feet, his bleary eyes registering the time—four thirty-two a.m.—on the bedside clock before he stumbled toward the nursery. He'd assured Ali he could cope with the night-time feeds and that she was to get a decent night's sleep but he'd had no idea just how fractured that would leave him. He rubbed his face wearily. He usually coped well on little sleep. It must be the jet lag catching up with him.

Ali's soothing voice came through the open nursery door as he approached.

"Hey," he said softly. "I'm sorry. I didn't mean for him to wake you."

"It's okay," she said, turning to him with a smile, the baby squalling in her arms. "I was already awake."

His eyes raked over her. Her tumbled dark curls, the faint crease on her cheek that must have come from her pillow. The shadows of her curves beneath her night-gown. His body reacted without a second thought, his senses coming to swift attention even as his ears continued to be filled with the baby's cries. This situation shouldn't be having this effect on him, he told himself, and yet he could barely tear his eyes from Ali.

He realized he was staring and forced himself to move. "Let me get his bottle, and then you can go back to bed."

His tongue thickened on the words. *Back to bed.* Three simple words and yet they opened a floodgate on his memories, filling his mind with images of what they'd shared. Of what he wanted to share with her again.

"Thanks," Ali said, turning to change Joshua's diaper.

He forced his feet in the direction of the kitchenette that formed part of the nanny suite. Forced his mind back to more mundane things. When he returned with the bottle she was settling into the rocking chair with the baby in her arms. The soft glow of the night-light bathed her in a golden wash of color. There was nothing mundane about Alison Carter in a nightgown. Nothing at all.

"I'll take him," he offered.

"It's okay. This shouldn't take too long. Besides, you look dead on your feet."

He handed her the bottle and leaned in the doorjamb watching as she fed his little nephew. Once Joshua was done, she wrapped him and put him back in his bassinette.

"You could have gone back to bed," she said gently as she closed the nursery door behind them.

"I was up, too."

She looked up at him, and her breath seemed to catch in her throat at what he knew was reflected in his eyes. Hunger. Desire. Need. Ali took a step away from him, and then another.

"I'll…um…I'll see you later in the morning, then," she said, turning away from him and back toward the nanny suite.

"Yeah, later."

He watched her go, tamping down the little voice in the back of his mind that urged him to follow her. To reach out and turn her to face him. To draw her into his arms and against his aching body and to do with her all the things his flesh clamored for.

"Ali?"

She hesitated a step, and then stopped.

"Yes?"

Words froze on the tip of his tongue.

"Ronin? Are you okay?"

No, he wasn't okay. He was jet-lagged and he was still staggering under the weight of his responsibilities—both old and new. He wanted more than anything in the world to lose himself in the oblivion he knew he'd find in her arms. But he knew he'd scare her away for good if he pressed her now.

"I'm glad you're here. Sweet dreams."

"Sweet dreams?" she answered, a quizzical look lifting one brow.

"Yeah."

Walk back to me, he silently begged her. Instead she gave him a sweet smile.

"You, too."

He stood there until he heard her bedroom door close, until he knew for certain that she wasn't going to change her mind and come to him. He returned to the master suite and threw himself down on his bed, his mind and his body too alert now for sleep to come back easily. She was resisting the attraction between them, but she felt it as strongly as he did. He knew it as well as he knew the stubbled reflection that greeted him in the bathroom mirror every morning. It didn't make sense. He thought back to the instant sizzle of awareness that had struck them back in Hawaii and how quickly they'd both given in to it.

The sizzle was still very definitely there, but she was fighting it. Was it because he now came with a child as part of the package, or was there something else that was holding her back? He didn't know right now but his specialty was solving puzzles. It would only be a matter of time before he solved hers, he promised himself as he rolled over onto his side and forced his eyes closed.

It was harder than she'd expected to fight the allure of the two males under the same roof as her over the next two days. There was something about seeing

Ronin with his nephew that plucked at her emotions until her attraction to him was near impossible to resist. Whether it was watching him bathe the baby, or use his large hands to scoop the wriggling wee tadpole from the bathwater and gently towel him dry, she couldn't help but be mesmerized.

She shifted a little in Ronin's chair and tried to focus on her laptop screen. He'd suggested she work in his office so she'd be less likely to be interrupted, but the entire time she was in there all she could think about was him. His office held an eclectic collection of things that reflected the type of man he was. A scale suspension bridge filled a table to one side of the desk—apparently a replica of a job in South America his firm was consulting on at the moment. When she'd asked if he needed to go there like he had to Vietnam recently, he'd shaken his head and informed her he didn't plan to do any overseas travel for at least the next six months.

His words had surprised her. From what she'd been able to glean so far, a big part of his work had included overseas travel, but now he seemed to have changed all that. The fact he was taking his duty to Joshua so seriously was just another facet to him that warmed her in places that had no business being warmed. Not when she was going to be leaving here, leaving them, first thing on Monday morning.

She thought about the past two days sharing the baby's care. They had fallen into an all-too-comfortable routine. Ronin would get up with the baby in the morning and leave her to catch up on email and make all necessary calls. By the time she was done, the baby was usually waking from his morning sleep and ready for another bottle. Now Joshie was getting the hang of things, he was turning into a voracious feeder—a fact which caused an equally vigorous output in other areas, which had horrified Ronin to no end. The rest of the day they shared his care around their own work commitments and even enjoyed some time with the three of them together.

For Ronin it had been simple—he'd delegated all but the most urgent of matters to his team. Even for Ali things had gone more smoothly than she'd imagined. In fact, Deb had even asked if they could keep the woman she referred to in her daily updates as Mrs. Fix-It.

When all was said and done, though, Ronin was coping well and, with the news that his mother would be released from hospital over the weekend, things were definitely improving. The agency had confirmed the nanny roster would begin, as originally planned, from Monday. Only two more nights, Ali assured herself, and she'd be able to get her life back on track. In fact, there really was no reason for her to continue to stay through to Monday. Ronin had slid into the role of Joshua's carer so competently he really didn't need her any more. Maybe she should talk to him about that, she mused, before dragging her attention back to her computer screen.

She hit Send on the email she'd just written to a new client and leaned back in her chair. Technically she shouldn't even be working on a Saturday. She looked outside. It was raining. It wasn't as if there was any motivation to head out for a brisk walk, which was a shame since she'd been neglecting her usual daily exercise while she'd been here. Maybe she'd ask Ronin if she could use his gym for an hour or so.

The door behind her opened.

"Coffee?" Ronin asked from behind her.

Ali could smell the brew and she swiveled the chair around to face him.

"Thank you."

She took the mug he offered, their fingers brushing as she did so. It didn't matter how often they touched, or how accidentally—the result was always the same. Her heart rate would speed up, her breath would quicken and the spot where they'd connected would tingle for a few seconds. It was growing harder and harder to resist him. Even her nights were filled with dreams about what they'd shared back in Hawaii. She'd lost count of the number of times she'd woken, her heart pounding and her body straining for a release that never came.

"Joshie's gone down for a sleep," he said, hitching his butt against the edge of the desk beside her.

The heat from his body reached out to her, filling the space between them. Enticing her. Daring her to move closer. Ali stood—or, more accurately, sat—her ground.

"That's early," she commented, before taking a long sip from the steaming mug warming her hands.

With the rain had come a bitter southerly wind, and temperatures had definitely dropped.

"Yeah, maybe it's the weather."

"Speaking of the weather, I had planned to go for a jog today, but with the rain, that's not going to happen. I was wondering if I could use your gym for a while."

"Of course. You don't need to ask. You have the run of the place."

"Great. It's just down the end of this hall, isn't it?"

"Yeah, let me show you," he said, putting his coffee mug down on the desk and heading for the door.

She followed him out of the office and down the hall. He opened the door to usher her into his multi-gym, complete with a leg press, a stand stacked with free weights, a treadmill and an elliptical trainer, all of which showed he was serious about fitness. Not that she didn't know that already. She'd examined almost every inch of his well-sculpted form once before. A girl didn't forget details like that.

"Are you familiar with all of this?" he asked.

"Most of it," she said, dragging her attention back to his question, "although I'll probably just use the tread-mill for half an hour or so. It's been a while since I've done any proper exercise."

"Use whatever you want," he offered.

"Great, thanks. I'll go get changed."

It only took a few minutes to slip into her running gear and then she was back in the gym. To her sur-prise, Ronin had changed into a loose-fitting singlet and shorts, and was shifting an impressive set of weights on the leg press.

"I thought I'd follow your example and grab some exercise while I can," he said as she crossed the room to the treadmill. "I've brought the monitor in here with us."

"Oh, good idea," she said.

Her eyes danced over the muscles in his long legs as he worked through a series of repetitions. She flung him a distracted smile before mounting the treadmill and adjusting the settings to start a slow, steady run. She began to pound out the kilometers, trying to keep her gaze averted as Ronin went through a routine of weight training and exercises. But it was impossible to ignore the power in his shoulders as he did a set of lat-eral pull-downs. Power she'd felt beneath her fingertips.

A buzz started up in her body that had nothing to do with the endorphins that should be starting to build up about now. She forced her eyes away from him again and focused on her breathing. When that didn't work she increased the incline on the treadmill. Anything that would keep her attention on herself and away from the man working out only a couple of meters away from her.

A trickle of sweat worked its way down her spine, heightening her sensitivity. Still she pushed herself. Still to no avail. Ronin had moved to lay down on the bench press, his legs straddling the bench as he reached for the bar. Unbidden, an image of her straddling him, right here, right now, burned across her retinas.

A shaft of longing pierced her, so sharp and so swift she stumbled a little on the treadmill mat.

"You okay?" Ronin asked.

"Sure, I'm fine," she said breathlessly. "Just a bit out of condition."

"You look pretty fine from where I am," he teased with a smile.

She was anything but fine. Every cell in her body cried out for her to act on her fantasy. For her to strip herself of the tight-fitting Lycra top she wore and to press her heated skin against his. She pushed against the rise of desire that swelled through her, but it pushed back twice as hard.

This was hopeless. She'd have been better off running outside in the driving rain and chilling wind. She lowered the incline a notch and dialed back the speed a little. The sooner this was over the sooner she could get out of the room and head for a shower. A very cold one. By the time her half hour was up her legs felt like jelly, and it had nothing whatsoever to do with the run she'd just completed. Ronin, having finished his set, sat up to wipe his face with a towel. Sweat soaked his singlet, making it cling to the sculpted contours of his body.

Ali swallowed hard against the sudden dryness in her throat.

"There are water bottles in the little fridge over there in the corner," Ronin said, gesturing with a nod of his head.

"Uh, thanks."

She walked past, struck by the heat wave that flowed around him. Sweaty male had never been her thing—in fact, she'd never understood the appeal when friends had giggled over some guy or another at the gym—but she got it now, all right. Her inner muscles clenched with a primal response to the intensity and strength that emanated from him, and she felt her breasts grow heavy and begin to tingle.

Eager for any distraction, she opened the small fridge tucked in the corner and swiped two bottles from the door. She tossed one in Ronin's direction before opening hers and taking a long drink.

"Feeling better now?" Ronin asked.

"Better?"

"You're clearly used to exercising, and with looking after Joshua for me I guess you haven't been able to work out like you would normally. I know I get antsy when I can't work out."

That wasn't the only thing she hadn't done in a while. The thought pinged through her mind so strongly that for a moment she was worried she'd actually said it out loud. Ronin still looked at her, clearly awaiting her reply.

"Yeah, I know what you mean. It felt good to run."

"Ever tried mountain biking?"

She shook her head. "That's for people more intrepid than I," she said with a rueful smile.

Ronin laughed softly. "You should try it sometime. The Whitford forest runs behind the house and into the valley. It has some great trails."

"No, I don't think so. I like my bones intact."

She regretted her words the moment she'd said them, as they became a catalyst for Ronin to sweep his gaze over her body. She felt it physically—as if it were a long caress—and her body reacted instantly. Her breasts, already sensitive, felt almost painfully constricted beneath her sports bra, and a deep throb pulsed at the apex of her thighs. She took another sip of water, this time spilling some of the liquid, a droplet running off her chin and down her chest to the shadowed cleft at the neckline of her fitted top.

Ronin's eyes darkened as they followed the track of that single drop. Ali knew she should do something. Move. Anything. But she was held hostage to the look on his face, the burning hunger in his gaze. When he stood and took a step toward her, she felt a bolt of electricity zap through her. The heat she'd felt pouring off him before was nothing compared to the scorching temperature that sizzled between them now.

Nine

Ronin slid the towel from around his neck and lifted it toward her.

"Here," he said, his voice thick, as though even words were too much at this point.

She watched his long strong fingers, tan against the white cotton of the towel, as he dabbed at the moisture on her chest. Then, whether by accident or design, his knuckle grazed against her skin. She dragged in a ragged breath at his touch. Again she reminded herself to move. To step away. To remove herself from the temptation that this man presented. Again she remained rooted to the spot.

The towel slid from his grasp and fell to the floor at their feet. He ignored it, instead tracing the swell of her breast with the backs of his fingers. Despite the heat that threatened to make her combust right here, goose bumps peppered her skin at his caress.

"You're so beautiful," he said, his voice a rumble from deep in his chest.

She couldn't respond. Her heart was pounding like a mad thing and it took all her concentration just to be able to breathe. When he bent his head toward her, it was pure instinct that responded. Not reason, not common sense—no, it was need, pure and simple. She was so desperate now for his touch, his heat. Her body ached.

His lips took hers hungrily, his tongue a welcome intrusion. She pressed against him and rocked against his arousal, earning a groan of torment from him in reply. It did nothing to relieve the demand that built deep inside her—it only served to stoke the flames that licked her body. When Ronin's hands went to the bottom edge of her top and began to peel it off, she lifted eager hands to assist him. Then, as his fingers deftly unsnapped the hooks of her sports bra, she pulled it from her shoulders, exposing her breasts to his hungry gaze and, even better, his hungry mouth.

A spear of need pierced her as he dragged one nipple into his mouth and sucked hard. Her legs weakened, but he held her upright as he feasted first on one breast, then the other. Ali's fingers tightened on his broad shoulders, her nails embedding a row of tiny crescents in his skin. Somewhere in the back of her mind she knew she should stop him, stop this before it went too far, but she craved him with a longing that went soul deep. She couldn't deny it, not anymore.

When he released her, she wobbled on her legs. For a second she was confused, not understanding, but then she felt his hands at the waistband of her running shorts—felt him pull them, together with her panties, down over her hips to tangle at her feet. Then he was on his knees before her, his breath a heated rush against the tender skin at the top of her thighs. His hands reached around her to splay across her buttocks, to tilt her closer to him. Her sex felt swollen, and the pulse that had built up before grew to a pounding beat.

He nuzzled her, making a shudder ripple in a giant wave through her body. She leaned back against the front rail of the treadmill, her arms reaching behind on either side, desperately searching for an anchor. With relief she found and gripped hold of the rail as Ronin's tongue swept across her. Spears of pleasure shot from her center. Ali could barely stand and she tried to ease her feet further apart but, manacled as they were by her shorts, she was captive to his whim.

She caught sight of her reflection in the mirrored wall opposite. Her cheeks were flushed, her breasts thrust forward by her grip on the equipment behind her. Her nipples were tight dark pink bullets, and every muscle in her torso was rigid. She looked lower, to the dark blond head, the strong neck and the broad shoulders that tapered to Ronin's narrow waist. The vision before her blurred as he stroked her again and again with his tongue, his hands kneading her buttocks in silent rhythm with his mouth, his stubbled jaw rasping against her inner thighs. And then he closed his lips around her most sensitive point, his teeth gently grazing the nub of exquisitely responsive nerve endings, and sucked hard.

Her orgasm swept through her, wave after escalating wave of pleasure swamping her senses. She let go of the rails and, with his guidance, sank to the floor, vaguely aware of him pulling her shoes and socks from her feet and untangling her clothing until she lay naked on the carpet before him. With swift, sure movements he tugged off his singlet and kicked off his footwear before carefully removing his shorts.

His erection jutted, thick and proud, from the nest of curls at his groin. Ali reached for him, her fingers closing around the silken length of his shaft, stroking him firmly. His eyes closed and he shook as she repeated the action. When he opened his eyes again they were burning blue flames, burning for her.

"I want you so badly," he said, through gritted teeth, "but if you don't want this, say it now."

In answer, Ali positioned him at her wet swollen entrance, her eyes locked on his. "I want this," she whispered, as she lifted her hips to feel the blunt tip of him nudging her slick folds. "I want *you*."

Without a second's hesitation Ronin surged forward, filling her completely and triggering a new raft of sensation deep inside. Ali gasped with the wonder of it all, her legs locking around his hips as he rocked against her. She was oblivious to the roughness of the carpet beneath her, her entire being focused solely on the man who surged above and within her, again and again until her body responded with renewed vigor and tumbled once more over the precipice and into the realms of delight.

Her hands gripped his shoulders, shoulders that were taut with tension, as he drove into her, seeking his own release. Suddenly he withdrew and groaned as his seed spilled across her belly. Beneath her hands she felt him shudder, felt his muscles begin to relax.

He reached for the towel he'd dropped—was it only minutes before? It felt like so much longer. Carefully, he wiped her clean.

"I'm sorry, I didn't think—" he started.

"It's okay," she interrupted. "We're safe."

Bowled over by their desire, neither of them had given a thought to contraception. She couldn't tell him that it wouldn't have made any difference. That no matter what method he'd used, pregnancy was not an option. The reminder hit her with a stinging cold dose of reality.

Ali eased away from him, unable to look him in the eye. As intimate as they'd been, right now she needed distance. Right on cue, a cry sounded from the baby monitor Ronin had placed on the shelf earlier. She hurried to her feet, grabbing her clothing from the floor and clutching it to her.

"I'll see to him," Ronin offered. "You go shower."

She gave him a nod of acceptance, relieved to be able to put some distance between them. Dressed, he'd always been a temptation. Naked, he was nigh on irresistible. But she couldn't afford to go there again. Couldn't lower her defenses. Not when she knew she would only prove to be a disappointment to him in the long run.

His words of only a few short weeks ago, that he'd always imagined he'd fill his house with a family, echoed in her mind. While she could give him everything that was within her, it would never be enough. Giving him a family was the one thing at which she would always fail.

Ronin pulled on his sweat-dampened clothing with a grimace and grabbed the monitor before leaving the gym. He should be buzzing with satisfaction right now and yes, physically he felt sated. But mentally he felt like Ali had taken several giant steps away from him, and he was at a complete loss as to why. Joshua's cries became more demanding. He could hear him in stereo now, Ronin realized as he neared the downstairs sitting room and turned down the monitor in his hand. Figuring out what had just gone wrong with Ali would have to wait for another time.

A few minutes later he eyed the baby's diaper with distaste.

"Gee, thanks, mate," he muttered to the little boy who, now diaperless, gleefully kicked his legs. "You couldn't have left this one for Ali?"

He quickly cleaned up the mess and rediapered the little guy before lifting him and propping him against his shoulder.

"I guess you're ready for some lunch, huh? Steak and eggs? Poached salmon and wilted spinach? No? How about a bottle then?"

He gently put his nephew in the baby bouncer and went to wash his hands and prepare Joshie's bottle. He went through the motions automatically, all the while trying to sort through the niggle of unease that still bothered him about Ali. She'd been a willing partner in what they'd just shared, he knew that for a fact. He'd given her an out, and not only had she refused it, she had given every indication of wanting him just as badly as he'd wanted her. How he'd ever found the presence of mind not to come inside her was nothing short of a miracle.

And what if he had? he wondered. To his surprise he couldn't push the idea of what might have happened next from his mind. In fact, a sense of warmth filled him at the idea of having children with Ali. He shook his head as Joshua squawked in protest at how long he was taking to ready the baby's feed. One step at a time, he thought as he scooped the little boy back up into his arms and offered him the bottle. One step at a time.

He was just burping the baby when Ali came into the kitchen. He didn't know whether she was attempting to keep him at bay or was genuinely feeling cold, but the jeans and loose-fitting turtleneck skivvy she wore shrieked "hands off."

"Everything okay?" she asked. "I tried to be as quick

as I could. I imagine you're starting to feel a bit cold dressed like that?"

Ronin hadn't even noticed the temperature, but now she mentioned it his damp gym gear did feel a bit uncomfortable. "It's okay."

"Here, do you want me to take him so you can go and get cleaned up?"

Even her voice sounded distant. At a time when they should have been closer than ever, she'd cloaked herself with the speed of the *U.S.S. Enterprise* anticipating a Klingon attack.

"Regrets?" he asked, determined to get to the point of her distance. He could fix this—he was sure of it—if she would just tell him what was wrong.

Her eyes flared wide at his question. She shook her head and looked down at the table, tracing an imaginary pattern on its surface as she allowed her hair to swing forward and block her expression from his view. She sighed.

"No," she finally answered, her voice small.

"Then what's the problem? We're two consenting adults, aren't we?"

She dragged in another ragged breath before answering. "Yes, last time I looked."

"Then there's *nothing* wrong."

"As long as we both agree it was just a pleasant interlude and no more," she said, lifting her head to look at him.

"What else could it be?" he asked, fighting back the urge to ask why she was so determined to dismiss the special connection they shared. For goodness sake, he was thirty-five years old. He'd been around the block a few times, certainly enough to know that the sparks they struck off one another were more than sheer luck.

Joshua chose that moment to belch loudly, showering Ronin's shoulder with a warm, wet dampness that told him that as much as he'd like to pursue this conversation with Ali a little further, now really wasn't the time.

"You're right," he said, handing over his wee charge. "I need to take a shower and get dressed."

She took the baby without a word and wandered over to the couch, where she sat down with him tucked into the crook of her arm. He watched as Ali picked up a baby book with her free hand and began thumbing through the pages, reading the story to Joshua as she went.

They'd just been as intimate as a couple could be, and still she was keeping her distance. Frustration unfurled within Ronin's mind. Why couldn't he get past her barriers? It was like trying to piece together a puzzle while blindfolded. No matter which way he turned or which angle he used to approach her, she continued to retreat. Should he just give up and let her walk away?

He turned and left the room and pounded up the stairs to his master suite. After he stripped off, he stepped into his voluminous shower stall and turned on the pulsating cascade of water. He braced his arms against the shower wall and bent his head beneath the stream, letting it rush over him and soak away the tension that had built so quickly. Life was so short, so precious. Losing his sister and her husband had proven that. That tragedy was making him reevaluate things on a daily basis. He thought again about the question he'd asked himself downstairs. *Should I just give up and let Ali walk away?*

The answer that echoed through his mind was a resounding *no*. He wasn't ready to give up yet.

Ten

By Sunday morning the stormy weather had blown away to reveal a typical Auckland late-autumn blaze of sunshine. As Ali made her way downstairs to the kitchen for breakfast, she thanked her lucky stars that today marked her last full day here with Ronin. After yesterday's weakness, she doubted she'd be able to hold out against him much longer if he made overtures to her again.

Ronin was already downstairs with Joshua. She watched from the door for a while as he interacted with the baby, and it made her heart ache to see them. To see Joshie's blue eyes fix on Ronin as he held the baby in his arms and talked a barrel load of nonsense to him.

"Good sleep?" he asked, looking up at her when he realized she was standing there.

"Okay," she said, not prepared to admit just how disjointed her rest had been, filled as it was by reenactments of their gym encounter.

"I need to ask you for a favor today," Ronin continued, putting Joshua into his bouncer and jiggling the attached mobile. "Would you mind looking after this little man while I help Dad bring Mum home from the hospital?"

"Sure. How long do you think you'll be?"

Not that it mattered, because she'd promised she'd stay until the next day, anyway.

"A couple of hours with Mum and Dad, I guess, but then I have to go to CeeCee and R.J.'s house. I have to remove their personal effects so the other contents can be auctioned and the property can be listed for sale. Will you be okay?"

She nodded. Hadn't she single-handedly cared for the baby when he'd been released from hospital already?

"Sure, take however long you need. We'll be fine here."

He gave her a grateful smile. "Thanks, I really appreciate it. I'd have left Dad to mind Joshua but it'd be too much for him with Mum coming home as well. He's had enough on his plate."

And what about you? Ali asked silently. *Haven't you shouldered the responsibility for everyone, without question? Who's been there for you?* There'd only been her, and she was counting the minutes until she could leave. A pang of guilt struck her. Maybe she'd read too much into yesterday, thinking he was looking to start a relationship that she knew she couldn't handle. Maybe he'd just been seeking surcease in sensation. Maybe it wouldn't have made a difference if it had been her or some other woman he knew and was attracted to.

The second the thought came to her mind, an irrational wave of jealousy hit her. She groaned inwardly. This was ridiculous. Second-guessing herself all the time was one thing, second-guessing how Ronin's mind worked was a road she certainly didn't want to tread. Besides, she rationalized as she poured some cereal into a bowl and added milk, the nanny rotation started from tomorrow and everything would run like clockwork without her. He wouldn't need her at all.

"What time are you heading out?" she asked, fighting back the completely irrational twinge she'd felt at the fact he wouldn't need her.

"As soon as I can. I'll collect Dad on the way to the hospital."

"You do what you need to do. Joshua and I will manage perfectly," she said, a smile firmly pasted on her mouth.

And they did manage perfectly. Aside from a short-lived cranky episode in the late afternoon—a time Ali remembered her sisters referring to as Arsenic Hour—the day had gone well. But it was well dark before Ali heard the garage door roll open and then, after a few moments, heard Ronin's weary steps come down the hallway from the garage to the kitchen.

She looked up from the table where she'd been sitting with her laptop and was shocked to see how gray Ronin looked. Weariness had scored deep lines between his brows and his eyes, usually flashing with brilliance, looked dull and unhappy.

"Hi," she said, unsure of how to ask him how his day had gone. "You've just missed seeing Joshua. I put him down ten minutes ago."

"No doubt I'll see him during the night," Ronin said, with a weight in his voice she'd never heard before.

"I kept a meal for you. It's warming in the oven."

"Thanks," he said, turning to the oven and reaching for his plate.

"Look out—it's hot!" she warned, moving to her feet and across to the oven to pass him an oven mitt.

"Sorry. Wasn't thinking."

"That's okay. They're *your* fingers. Look, why don't you sit down and I'll bring this over to you?"

"I'm not helpless," he argued.

"I didn't say you were," she consoled. "Now, go. Sit."

She deftly slipped on the mitt and pulled his plate from the oven shelf and popped it on the bench. Once Ronin sat at the table, she lay out cutlery in front of him, then went to the bench and grabbed a half bottle of red wine he'd left there the night before and poured him a glass.

When she plunked the glass in front of him, he looked up with a crooked smile.

"Do I look like I need this?"

"Yes, you do. Frankly you look like you need hard liquor, but since I don't know where you keep your whiskey, this will have to suffice," she answered, and then went to peel the aluminum foil off his plate and deliver it to the table.

She poured herself a glass of wine, too, and joined him at the table. She watched as he used his fork to shift the braised lamb shank with kumara mash around on his plate.

"No good?" she asked. "I can put some mac and cheese together if you'd rather."

Mac and cheese had always been her mother's staple comfort offering, Ali remembered, when one of her girls had had a tough day. And Ronin looked as if he'd had a very tough day.

"No, it's fine. Better than fine," he said, and ate a few

mouthfuls before putting his fork down and pushing the plate away from him. "I'm sorry. I can't do it justice."

"That's okay."

Ali went to remove the plate, but Ronin reached out and caught her by the wrist.

"It's not you or your cooking," he said, his voice strained. "It's just been a hellish day."

"Is your mother okay?"

"She's fine. Tired, which is understandable, but glad to be home again. It was being at my sister's house that really hit me hard. I thought the funeral had given me closure, you know? That now, a few weeks down the track, I'd be ready for this. I didn't realize how difficult it would be to be in their house, to go through their things, or to discover how much I miss her."

His voice cracked and, with that sound, the hard shell around Ali's heart did, too. She knew what loss felt like. What it did to you when the world you knew ceased to turn on its axis anymore. When everything shattered and you were left with your life in pieces you had no idea how to put back together.

"I'm sorry," he continued, letting her go. "I shouldn't off-load onto you."

"It's okay," she said quietly. "And—trust me on this—if you don't off-load onto someone, eventually it will consume you."

He looked up from the table, his eyes bleak and empty. "I'm glad you're here, Ali."

Ronin stood and took his plate over to the kitchen bench. He scraped his uneaten food into the trash before stacking his plate and utensils in the dishwasher.

"Look, I'm beat. I think I'll take this—" he snagged his glass of wine "—and head off for an early night."

"Good idea," Ali said. "I'll see you in the morning."

She stayed downstairs a little longer, sipping her wine and looking out the French doors toward the lights that glittered in the distance like glow worms on a black canvas. This was her last night here. She should be positively gleeful at the prospect of returning to her world, her life, and yet somehow the edge had rubbed off her eagerness to leave. Why was that?

The answer came quite swiftly, and she rolled it round in the back of her mind before finishing her wine in a single gulp and putting her glass on the kitchen bench. She switched off the downstairs lights and headed for the stairs. At the top, she hesitated. Turn left toward her room, or turn right toward the master suite?

She turned right.

She'd never been into this part of the house before. Somehow, knowing it was Ronin's private domain had made it feel completely off-limits. Besides, she'd had no cause to come here. From the layout of the ground floor, she knew the master suite had to be large, but she hadn't realized it also included a very spacious sitting room. She took a deep breath and stepped through the double doors that opened into the sitting room. She could hear the sound of water running, then silence. Ali froze in her tracks. It wasn't too late to change her mind. She could leave now and he'd never know.

She turned, one hand on the door to retrace her steps, when across the sitting room a door opened. Ronin walked out, a white towel slung around his hips. A towel he'd barely used, judging by the droplets of moisture that still clung to his body.

Her eyes roamed his bare flesh, the damp matted scattering of hair at his chest, the trail that formed a line bisecting his lower belly.

"Ali?"

She dragged her gaze up to his face, to the confusion she saw there. Whatever she'd thought she could say to him fled her mind.

"Is Joshua okay?" Ronin asked, taking a few steps toward her.

She inhaled, readying herself to speak, but her senses were filled with the scent of him. With the cool sea air crispness of whatever soap he used blended together that that inimitable scent that was pure male, pure Ronin. "He—he's fine," she managed. "I just…I just wanted to make sure you're okay," Ali finished lamely.

Ronin's eyes darkened. "Okay?"

"Yeah, I…look, never mind."

She turned to leave, feeling ridiculous for having thought for a second she could go through with this. But then warm fingers caught at her hand and stopped her in her tracks. Slowly, ever so slowly, she turned back.

Ronin gave her a gentle tug toward him. Unresisting, she went, her hands flattening on the expanse of his chest.

"Ronin, I—"

She never managed to finish her sentence. The words she had been about to say fled. Her palms tingled and her fingers curled against his skin. She lifted her face to his and rose on tiptoe to capture his mouth with her own. Their kiss swept her away on a tide of longing. They were two wounded souls, each needing oblivion, a chance to forget.

When Ronin broke their embrace, a small cry of regret escaped her, but he took her by the hand and led her into the master bedroom. Soft lighting bathed the wide bed in a golden glow. Ronin tugged down the sheets with a few swift movements and then turned back to Ali.

"Here, let me," she said as his hands reached for her.

She quickly pulled off her sweater and unfastened her jeans before skimming them down her legs. She stepped out of her house shoes and the pooled denim at the same time and stood, dressed only in her apricot lace panties and bra.

Ronin reached for her again and she came into his arms, her skin warming instantly on contact with his. Her hands went to the towel at his waist, tugging firmly until it came loose, and she tossed it to one side. She gave him one brief, hard kiss and then pulled back.

"Sit," she commanded in a whisper. "No, lie down."

With a tiny smile pulling at his lips, he did as she said. Ali joined him on the bed, straddling his legs and placing her hands at his shoulders. Slowly she began to trace the outline of his muscles with her fingertips, working down his body—over the taut discs of his nipples, down his ribcage, lingering at his belly button. Beneath her touch his skin dotted with goose bumps. She followed each touch with a gentle swirl of the tip of her tongue until she heard him groan and felt his hands fist in her hair.

"Ali, stop. You don't have to do this," he gritted between clenched teeth.

"Let me be the judge of that," she said, looking up at him from beneath her lashes.

When his fingers relaxed a little, she continued on her path. He was fully aroused, his flesh a taut shaft against his lower belly. She traced the length of him, from base to tip with her fingers, and then with her tongue. His hips pushed upward, and beneath her legs she felt his thighs grow rigid. She teased the tip of her tongue around his swollen head before taking him into her mouth.

His sharply indrawn breath was his only acknowledgment as she pleasured him with her hands, her mouth, her tongue. As tension built in his body, she could feel him coiling tighter and tighter, determined to maintain control.

"I want to be inside you," he groaned. "Please, now."

She released him to fall wetly against his belly and rose to her knees.

"Condom," he said, reaching for a packet in his bedside drawer and tearing it open.

Ali took the sheath from him and took her own good time rolling it on. The entire time, he watched her, his eyes glittering like multifaceted sapphires. When he was covered, she raised herself over him and positioned him at her center. Slowly she took him into her body, relishing the tug and pull of flesh as he slid deeper and deeper again.

A ripple of pleasure rolled through her, making her clench her inner muscles around him and dragging another groan from his lips.

"Too much?" she asked with a half smile.

"Never," he declared, and reached for her hips, encouraging her to move.

As she slowly began to rock, Ronin thrust beneath her, his movements increasing the need that built and built until she felt him strain and push and cry out as his climax struck. She was so close, so close. She rocked against him, harder this time, faster, until she, too, felt the welcome swell of satisfaction swamp through her.

She lay down on his body, her head resting on his chest, and listened as his heart beat double time in her ear. Ronin traced lazy shapes on her back with his fingertips.

"Thank you," he said, his voice a rasp in the air.

"What for? You mean this?" she clenched around him again.

"No. For coming to me."

She lay there, silent for a while longer. Then she spoke. "You needed me."

And there it was. She'd admitted it to herself. He needed her, so she'd gone to him. She hadn't protected herself, her heart, as she'd promised she would. She'd put his needs above her own need to protect herself. And she couldn't bring herself to regret the choice, even though she knew she had just laid herself open for some serious trouble ahead. She wasn't the kind of woman who could just have sex with someone and walk away saying "Thanks for the memories."

Even in Hawaii she'd felt a link to Ronin that had led to her choice to sleep with him that first night—and that had left her feeling hurt and rejected when he'd vanished by the next morning. That link had grown stronger and deeper, and now it involved far more than just the two of them.

She hadn't wanted to love him, or even begin to love him, but she knew now that she was fighting a losing battle.

Ronin's hands splayed across her back, his palms warm and strong, and he rolled them both so they were lying side-by-side.

"I'll be right back. Don't move a muscle," he instructed as he slipped from the bed.

She should get up anyway, find her clothes and go back to her room. Except she didn't want to. Tonight she'd felt closer to Ronin than ever before. It was a terrifying prospect. She didn't have long to ponder—he was back within seconds. Had he sprinted the distance to and from the bathroom?

Back in bed, Ronin reached above him and hit a switch, plunging the room into darkness. Her eyes adjusted slightly, and she could almost make out his features in front of her.

"Stay," he said firmly, hooking one arm around her and pulling her to him. "Stay with me here. Don't go tomorrow. Please?"

It was the final word that broke her last barrier down. The knowledge that he needed her, wanted her. At least for now.

"Yes," she answered, placing a kiss on his chest, "I'll stay."

His arm tightened around her and she waited as his breathing slowed, as he drifted off into slumber. Her eyes burned in the dark. Leaving him, and she eventually would have to, would come soon enough. But for now, she'd take what she could and damn the consequences to her fragile heart.

Eleven

There were times, Ali decided on Monday morning, when working with your best friend really wasn't the smartest of ideas.

"Ali, honey, are you sure you're doing the right thing? I mean, helping the guy out when he couldn't get a nanny is one thing—but moving in with him?"

Ali took in a long breath and counted to five. "No, I'm not sure I'm doing the right thing, but I can't see myself *not* doing it. I want to be with him, Deb."

She met Deb's concerned gaze and cringed inside as the concern turned to pity.

"Does he know?"

"That I can't have kids?" Ali shook her head. "It hasn't come up, and besides, it's too soon to throw that into the conversation. We're still really getting to know one another."

"Which is all the more reason why you should keep

your distance for now, don't you think? You know, do things the old-fashioned way. Actually get to know one another before you live together?"

"Sarcasm really isn't your best trait," Ali sniped in return, then sighed. "Look, I'm sorry. I shouldn't take it out on you."

"Too right you shouldn't. But it's okay. I understand. He's one hell of a hunk of man, isn't he? So, he must be pretty good between the sheets, huh?"

Ali's blush gave Deb all the reply she was going to get. Deb stood up from behind the reception desk and gave Ali a hug.

"Hey, if he makes you happy then I'm all for it. I just need to know you'll take care of yourself, buddy. I don't want to see you hurt again. Not like before. Promise?"

"Don't worry," Ali replied, putting on as brave a face as she could muster. "I know how to protect myself."

The thing was, she *did* know how to protect herself, and yet she'd chosen not to. Instead, she'd decided to embrace their budding relationship, for as long as it lasted.

Throughout the day Ali found her mind straying from her work and back out to Whitford—to Ronin, more specifically. She wondered how the meeting with the first nanny had gone, and how Joshua was adjusting to his new caregiver. A stupid pang of envy hit her straight in the solar plexus at the thought of someone other than herself or Ronin providing Joshua with care and attention. And love? Yes, and love. She pushed the thought away. She'd find out how Joshua's morning had gone later on today. After she'd been to her place to collect more clothes and a few personal effects, she'd be back out at the house and seeing the new nannies in action, all of them, over the next few weeks.

The idea sent a tiny thrill through her. She'd risen early this morning, remade the bed she'd been using in the nanny's suite and, at Ronin's suggestion, had shifted the things she already had with her into the second walk-in wardrobe in his room. Plonking her toothbrush into the holder on the marble bathroom vanity had given her an unreasonable sense of belonging. That said, she wasn't hurrying to let go of the lease on her apartment just yet. She knew full well how nothing was a sure thing in this life.

Her apartment was exactly as she'd left it just over a week before, albeit with a fine surface coating of dust in evidence. It didn't take her long to clean up and pack. She had a sparse wardrobe, preferring to buy select quality pieces she could mix and match for work and a handful of cheaper items for casual wear. Her suitcase was hardly bulging when she did up the zipper and hefted it onto the floor.

Am I doing the right thing? she asked herself as she locked the apartment door behind her and took the elevator down to the underground parking level. Only time would tell.

The week went quickly. Ali had forgotten how it felt to have something to look forward to at the end of the working day. Settling into a routine had come very naturally. When Ali pulled her car into her allotted bay in the garage on Friday night, she realized that the sensation that filled her now was genuine happiness. A feeling she hadn't felt in so long that she'd almost been unable to identify it at first. The connecting door to the house opened, and Ronin stood in the doorway, waiting to greet her.

Her heart swelled at the sight of him. His business

shirt was open at the throat, his tie seemingly long since discarded, and his shirtsleeves were rolled up, exposing strong forearms dusted with dark blond hair. She hurried from the car. Her briefcase and the quotes she needed to work on tonight would have to wait. Right now she had another priority.

"Good evening," she said with a smile as she slid her hands around Ronin's waist and lifted her face for his kiss.

"It is now," he murmured.

His lips were firm against hers, and Ali let herself revel in his caress, every fiber in her body firing to instant life at his touch. As much as they'd pleasured one another all the nights that she'd spent in his bed, she still wanted more. She thanked her lucky stars that Ronin felt the same way. Each day, each hour, each minute in his company had grown more precious than the last, and Ali had forced herself to admit that she was hopelessly and irrevocably in love.

Ronin pulled away and, taking her hand, led her through to the kitchen.

"Sit down," he said. "I'll pour you a glass of wine."

"You don't need to tell me twice," she said, walking through to the sitting room.

She sat on the sofa and slipped off her shoes before tucking her feet up underneath her. Ronin brought two glasses of red wine through and sat next to her, passing her one and then putting his arm around her shoulder to tug her closer. Outside, it started to rain. The northeasterly wind picked up and spattered droplets against the glass.

Ali snuggled against him, enjoying the solid feel of his strength and warmth at her side. It would be so easy to dream that this could be a forever thing. Despite the risk, she chose to ignore the fact that she was on borrowed time. Instead, she reveled in the here and now, savoring each precious memory and experience with Ronin, and with Joshie. She wasn't going to waste this moment, right here, right now.

"I saw my parents today," Ronin said, after taking a sip of wine. "They'd like to come out and visit on Sunday. You okay with that?"

"Sure, why wouldn't I be? How's your mum doing today? I'm amazed with her recovery."

Ronin had been in touch with his parents daily, visiting them at their home when he wasn't snowed under with work. His mother, Delia, had been making steady progress, which had been a great relief after all the family had been through. It reminded Ali again of how precious life was—of how you had to make the most of each moment, each opportunity presented to you, because it could be snatched away just as quickly as it had appeared.

"Going stir crazy stuck at home. Dad's doing his best, but I think they'd both benefit from an outing."

"Then let's plan a special lunch," Ali suggested.

"You sure you're okay with that?"

"Is there any reason I shouldn't be? I've met your father before and we got along okay." Another thought sprang to mind. "Are you worried your mum won't like me? Or that she'll disapprove? We haven't known each other long and she's bound to wonder about me living here."

Ronin squeezed her shoulders in response. "Not at all. She knows we're together. And for that, if nothing else, she'll love you."

* * *

His words didn't prevent Ali from being hopelessly nervous when Ronin's parents' car pulled up outside the house at eleven thirty a.m. on Sunday. As it turned out, she needn't have worried. Both Delia and her husband, Neil, were warm and friendly. Delia had gone so far as to envelop Ali in her arms and whisper a fervent "thank you" to her for being there when they needed help.

"I was only too glad to be able to," Ali replied.

"We'll be forever in your debt," the older woman whispered fiercely, tears springing to her eyes. Delia dabbed at the moisture with a tissue. "Oh go on, look at me. This is a happy occasion. Now, where's my grandson?"

"He's in the sitting room, waiting to see you," Ronin said with a smile. As his mother went into the house he bent his head to Ali's. "See? I told you she'd love you."

Ali just smiled as they followed his parents through to where Joshua lay sleeping in his bassinet.

"Oh, my," Delia cooed, "hasn't he grown? He looks so much like you and your sister did at that age. Don't you think so, Neil?"

Neil's expression said he pretty much thought all babies looked the same at a month old, but he murmured something indistinct in response. Ali watched him as he observed his wife. So much love and devotion shone from his eyes—Delia could have said the moon was made of blue cheese and he would have agreed, if it made her happy.

It was lovely to see their enduring affection, but it made her a little envious, too. After her divorce, she'd convinced herself she would never be the recipient of such steadfastness. And, until recently, she'd managed to convince herself that it didn't matter. That she had her growing business, her family—really, what more did she need? But, as she watched Ronin with his parents and his nephew—three generations gathered together, like so many of her own family's gatherings—it made her realize that she wanted so much more. That she wanted what they had.

If only it were possible.

Joshua chose that moment to wake up, delighting his grandmother with the opportunity to spoil him with attention until it was time for their lunch at one. The nanny came to take him back upstairs and Delia reluctantly let him go. They sat at the kitchen table to dine and Ali very proudly served up the meal she'd concocted after several hours of research on the internet yesterday. She'd been determined to follow as heart-friendly a menu as she possibly could, and her hard work had paid off.

It was as they were enjoying a coffee in the sitting room after lunch that Delia suddenly rose from her seat.

"Oh, heavens, I can't believe I forgot!" she exclaimed.

"Forgot what, Mum?" Ronin asked, rising also.

"I was going out of my mind with boredom this week, so I decided to put something together for Joshie—an album with photos of CeeCee and R.J. I know he's still far too young to appreciate it, so I was going to hold on to it until he was a bit older, but I thought you might like to take a look. I brought it with us, but left it in the car."

"That sounds like a lovely idea," Ali said with a smile as she gathered up their cups and saucers and stacked them on a tray to take out to the kitchen.

"I'll go and get it. Honestly, I can't believe I didn't bring it in with me. My memory seems to have taken quite a hit with this operation of mine."

"Don't worry, dear," Neil said, rising from the table

and putting his hands on his wife's shoulders to encourage her to regain her seat. "I'll get it from the car. Don't you worry about a thing."

"He's such a good man," Delia said as her husband left the room. "He's been my rock through all of this. I don't know what I'd have done without him."

"Dad's been your rock, but remember that you've always been his, too," Ronin said, settling down on the sofa beside his mother. "He needs you just as much as you need him."

"I still can't believe it," she said with an audible sniff. "That they're gone."

"I know, but we have to stay strong for Joshua. To keep them in his life."

"Yes, that's why I want him to grow up with the album—so they're familiar to him. So he can love them as much as we do," Delia said, fighting to gather her emotions back under control.

Ali felt the sting of sympathetic tears in her own eyes as she watched Ronin comfort his mother. To distract herself, she picked up the tray to take it out to the kitchen.

"You okay with that?" Ronin asked, looking up at her.

"I'm fine," she said behind a forced smile.

In the kitchen she gave Delia and Ronin a moment's privacy and busied herself stacking the dirty crockery in the dishwasher. By the time she returned to the sitting room, Neil had returned with the album and Delia had it on her lap.

"There you are, dear. I didn't want to start without you. It's a shame you never got to meet our CeeCee, or her husband, R.J. He'd been married before, you know, but his first wife never wanted children. CeeCee said that when she met him he was dreadfully unhappy, but our girl made him smile again."

Before Ali could comment, Delia was opening the cover and turning to the main page. Ronin started to get up from his seat beside his mother, but Ali waved him back down and perched on the arm of the sofa next to him.

"This is my favorite of all their wedding photos. Don't they just look so happy?" Delia smiled in reminiscence. "CeeCee told me later she'd just whispered to R.J. that they were having a baby. He was completely over the moon."

Ali leaned over slightly to get a better look at the page and instantaneously wished she hadn't. She hadn't expected to recognize the couple smiling happily, with eyes only for one another, nor did she expect to feel the sudden pain that ripped through her chest—as if her heart was being rent in two.

"Didn't they just make the most beautiful couple?" Delia asked.

But Ali couldn't answer, couldn't breathe. Couldn't believe she was staring at her ex-husband and his interior decorator. The woman he'd left her for. The woman who had borne him a baby.

Twelve

She must have murmured something in response to Delia's question, because Delia was now turning the pages—describing in detail why she'd chosen each picture for the scrapbook, lingering over the first ultrasound photo of Joshua, unwittingly driving a stake deeper and deeper into Ali's heart.

It wasn't that she still loved Richard—he'd destroyed that when he'd walked out on her for another woman—but she'd spent twelve years of her life with him. And he'd gone straight into the arms of a woman who'd been able to give him everything he'd ever wanted. Everything Ali had failed at. That little baby sleeping upstairs who she'd learned to love practically from the start was the son she'd never been able to give her husband. The son he'd had with another woman. The woman who, with Richard, had died only weeks ago. Ali couldn't believe he was dead. The awful finality of the word echoed in her mind. How could she not have known, not have heard somehow from anyone?

Delia finally closed the album. "And now little Joshie is the start of your family, Ronin. I'm so glad you're choosing to raise him yourself."

"It's what CeeCee and R.J. wanted," he said gruffly.

"But you'll be sure to give him brothers and sisters, won't you?" Delia pressed.

"All in good time, Mum. Let me come to grips with Joshua first," he laughed.

All in good time. Ronin's words signaled a death knell in Ali's mind to the relationship they'd just begun. Of course he'd want more children. She'd told herself that already. And they were the only thing she could never give him.

Ali operated on automatic for the balance of Neil and Delia's visit. She couldn't help but feel a deep sense of relief when Neil noticed his wife's energy levels were flagging and suggested they head home. After they'd waved them off, she and Ronin went back into the house.

"Are you okay?" Ronin asked. "You got really quiet there."

"A bit of a headache, that's all," Ali deflected.

"Why don't you put your feet up? I'll finish clearing up."

"It's all pretty much done," she answered. "But I think I might go and lie down for a bit."

His eyes narrowed in concern. "You're feeling that bad?"

Worse, she thought. But she couldn't tell him. Not now. Maybe not ever. He'd clearly adored his sister. How could she tell him that CeeCee had been the other woman in the breakup of her marriage?

"Do you need the doctor?" Ronin pressed.

"No, I'll be all right."

She went upstairs before he could say another word. In the master suite she walked through to the bathroom. She'd just closed the door behind her as the first sob fought its way out of her throat. Hard on its heels came another, and another. As she slid to the floor, the door at her back, she knew she wasn't mourning for her late ex-husband. She was mourning for what they'd never had—what she could never have with Ronin, what she'd been foolish to even attempt to reach for.

Delia's earlier words came back to haunt her. *His first wife had never wanted children.* How could Richard have said that? It was such a blatant untruth. She'd wanted to refute it, to scream that nothing had been further from the reality they'd shared. Why had Richard felt the need to lie about the reasons their marriage had failed? Was it perhaps because it had painted him and his relationship with CeeCee in a less than favorable light?

Whatever he'd been thinking, none of that mattered now. Richard was dead. Those three words repeated again and again in the back of her mind. And the bitter irony was that she now loved his son as if he were her own. The son of the woman who had inadvertently been the final chink in breaking apart the fragile armor of Ali's marriage. The pain that scored her now made her feel as if she was being betrayed all over again.

Richard. Married. Logically, Ali had known Richard had moved on with his life, but she'd made no effort to keep up with the details. Their friends had chosen sides, and she no longer kept in touch with anyone who was a significant part of Richard's life. There was no one to tell her about the wedding. But seeing those photos, seeing him happy in a way he hadn't been happy with her since the earliest days of their marriage, had been yet another blow. And it had made her current situation all the more clear.

Yes, Ronin was deeply attracted to her, and maybe he could even come to love her the way she knew she already loved him. But she knew that she couldn't count on that love to last, especially once her deficiency came to light. She didn't want to face that day, or watch what they'd started to build together be stripped away, layer by layer, until they had nothing left.

Ali buried her face in her knees and wrapped her arms tight around her lower legs, trying to make herself as small as possible. As if doing so could make the pain smaller, too. But it was useless. The pain kept on building until she knew there was only one thing left for her to do. She had to leave. She couldn't stay with the baby who was living proof of her shortcomings, or with the man she'd never be able to make lastingly happy. She had to stop this now before she gave Ronin false hopes. Before she set herself up for the silent recriminations that she'd already borne from another man.

She staggered to her feet and splashed some water on her face in an attempt to soothe the ravages of her misery, but the tears wouldn't stop coming. She grabbed a fistful of tissues from the vanity and walked through to the bedroom, throwing herself down on the bed and closing her eyes. Tomorrow. She'd leave tomorrow—that way she'd still have tonight. It would have to be a night to remember, because in her future, the memory would be all she had left.

Ronin moved quietly into the room. Ali lay asleep on the bed, still fully dressed and with her face turned in to her pillow. He grabbed a mohair blanket from the chest at the end of the bed and gently placed it over her before leaving the room again. Something was up. He knew it in his gut the same way he knew when something was going to go wrong with a contract. That was part of what made him so good at his job—being able to anticipate a problem before it became one. Having a working solution in his mind before it was required. Some people found his worst-case-scenario thinking to be downbeat, but he just called it risk management. Since he was totally risk averse, it had worked for him so far.

But with Ali, things had been different from the start. He had no worst-case scenarios worked out, no contingency plans in place. He'd gotten so swept up in her and the way she made him feel that all of his usual behavior had fallen by the wayside. Instead, he'd simply reveled in the sort of relationship he'd never expected to find in his tidy, orderly life. One that made him so simply and uncomplicatedly happy that he hadn't even considered that something could go wrong.

And that meant he had no idea how to fix things.

She wasn't something he could pick apart and peer through the layers to find out what was wrong. Even so, he racked his brain for what might have happened this afternoon to upset her, because despite her doing her best not to show it, he'd seen the pain reflected in her eyes and the tightness around her lips.

Was it something his mother had said? Was it the idea of having more children? No, it couldn't be that, he decided. It made no sense for her to be bothered by that. He'd seen Ali with Joshie. She loved him—it was there in every smile, every caress, every moment she spent with him. Her maternal instincts were right out there for anyone to see. Maybe it had been his quick rebuttal of his mother's suggestion that he give Joshie brothers and sisters in the near future? He tossed the thought around in his mind, examining it from every angle before putting it aside for now. Until he could get Ali to open up and tell him what she was thinking, anything else would merely be conjecture, and he knew that wouldn't get him where he needed to be.

He'd wait, keep an eye on her and figure out the problem. Then he'd fix it. Simple as that.

It was getting late when Ronin returned upstairs. The fact Ali still hadn't risen worried him. He'd made dinner and had waited for her to join him, putting her meal in the oven for her when she hadn't put in an appearance, then eventually wrapping it up and putting it away in the fridge. She'd even missed Joshua's evening bath and feed, something he knew she enjoyed sharing with him. Now the house was quiet.

He let himself into the master suite and checked on Ali. She was still in the same position she'd been when he'd left her. *That must have been some kind of headache.* With a faint sigh, he turned and went to the bathroom, stripping off his clothes as he went. He was standing at the vanity, contemplating a hot shower, when he saw a shadow of movement behind him in the mirror.

Ali. A sense of relief washed through him as her bare arms slid around his waist and he felt the heat of her body against his back. Relief quickly turned to something else as he realized she was, like him, naked.

"Feeling better?" he asked, searching her face in the mirror. There were still shadows in her eyes and she was a little pale, but she gave him a half smile. "You had me worried there," he continued.

"Nothing to worry about," she said simply.

"You missed dinner."

She pressed a kiss to the center of his spine that sent a bolt of longing straight to his groin. "I'm not hungry. Not for food, anyway."

She kissed a trail from between his shoulder blades to the small of his back. He turned around and pulled her up against him.

"Are you sure you're okay?"

"How about a bath?" she asked, avoiding his question. "I could do with a good soak."

He watched, slightly puzzled by her avoidance, as she sauntered to the raised steps that led to the marble spa bathtub he rarely used. Puzzlement fled as she bent over to turn on the faucet, adjusting the mixer until the water was at the right temperature. His body grew tight, his mind feeding his arousal with thoughts of how she'd look, slick with soap and lying in the warm water. Of how she'd feel beneath his hands.

He crossed the short distance between them and reached out to touch her, to cup the shape of her sweet buttocks and to run his hands down over her thighs as he pulled her back against his arousal.

"In a hurry?" she teased as she squirmed against him.

"For you, always," he replied, skimming his hands over her hips and her belly, and filling his palms with her breasts.

He rubbed his thumbs over her nipples, felt them shrink and grow tight under his touch. The bath filled with water and she reached for his wrists, gently easing his hands from her body and pulling him behind her up the steps to the bath. She let go of him as she entered, enticing him once again with the curve of her buttocks as she reached for a dish of bath salts and sprinkled them liberally through the water.

A spicy scent rose on the steam, which curled lazily

in the air around them. Ali sat down at one end of the bath and motioned for him to sit down in front of her. Game for whatever she suggested, he did exactly that.

Ali reached for the faucet and turned the water off, then pumped some liquid soap into her hands and began to wash his shoulders and his back. Her fingers slid over him. The touch felt exquisite, as always, but it wasn't nearly what he wanted. She reached around him with soapy hands and drew circles on his chest, drawing closer and closer to his nipples, pinching them gently between thumb and forefinger before sliding her hands deeper into the water.

Ronin's eyes slid shut as she closed her hand around his length, as she let her fingers clench and release as they worked their way to his tip and then back down again. He shuddered with the effort it took to hold back, to not give himself over to what she was doing, but he was determined to make sure she joined him on the same journey.

"Enough," he growled, mimicking her earlier action and grasping her gently by her wrists and pulling her hands away.

He was so hard, so ready, that it hurt. All he wanted to do was give in to his body's demand, but something still niggled at the back of his mind. Something that told him things weren't quite right.

"My turn," he said, shifting in the bath until he'd turned around and faced her.

Ronin pulled her forward, adjusting her legs so they bracketed his hips. Ali gripped the sides of the bath as he lathered up his hands and starting with her hands, began to work his way slowly up her arms. He took his time working the soap over her shoulders, along her collarbones, then down to her breasts, which rose, proud and full, just above the water line. He loved the feel of his hands on her skin, loved the sight of the contrast between his dark tan and her more golden hue. Again and again he circled his fingers closer to her nipples, and again and again he retreated.

A small frown appeared between her brows and her eyes narrowed as she looked at him.

"I never took you as a man who liked to torture a person," she said.

Despite the accusing words, her voice was thick with desire, music to his ears.

"I understand patience is a virtue," he teased, scooping up handfuls of warm water and allowing it to drizzle down over her chest, washing the bubbles away.

A tiny smile pulled at her lips. "So they say," she answered, her voice growing tight as he pumped more soap in his hands and began to wash her stomach. "I guess I'll just have to wait and find out."

"That you will," he promised, letting his hands drift lower, over the gentle swell of her belly to her hips, and then along the inside curve of her upper thighs.

She gasped as he stroked the tender skin on the inside of her legs, her body stiffening, waiting for his touch to become even more intimate. Ronin smiled and kept his eyes firmly on hers, locking her with his gaze, daring her to break it. He kept his touch light and teasing, watching as her pupils dilated, as her cheeks flushed pink with desire.

Seeing her response played havoc with his body. His erection strained between them, aching to be buried in that special place where his fingers tantalized and tangled. Ali's breaths grew shorter, her eyes now glazing, but still she held that connection between their gazes. When he firmed his touch, sliding first one, then a second finger inside her while stroking her clitoris with his thumb, her lips parted in a frantic pant. Still she looked into his eyes.

He'd never shared this depth of bond with another person. To have them laid open to him like this, trusting him implicitly. He curled his fingers and stroked her again, driving a deep moan from her. Encouraged, he repeated the action, and again and again until he saw the rise of color spread across her body, felt the contraction of her inner muscles against his fingers, saw her eyes slide shut. And watched as she dropped her head back and gave herself over to sensation.

Ronin gently withdrew his hand and rose in the water, reaching to scoop her up into his arms. Carefully he stepped from the bath and crossed to his bedroom, uncaring that they dripped water across the carpet as he put her, soaking wet, on the bedcovers. He quickly found a condom and tore it from its packet, covering himself with swift efficiency before positioning himself between her legs.

Ali lifted her hips to welcome him, her arms reaching for him and closing around his neck to hold him tight. He guided his erection inside her slowly, relishing the miracle of her slick and swollen flesh. *This,* he thought, giving himself over to the now primal demand of his body, *is where I want to be. Where I belong. With her. Forever.* When his climax hit, it hit hard and felt as if it would have no end.

Thirteen

Ali woke an hour before dawn. She was curled up in Ronin's arms, sheltered by his strength. She inhaled, wanting to lock this moment, this memory, the very scent of his skin, in her heart forever.

Sometime during the night, Ronin had discarded the damp bedcovers and pulled the sheet and some extra blankets over them, but not before they'd made love again. In the darkness their joining had been so poignant it had brought tears to her eyes, and she'd been thankful for the mantle of shadows that night had given her, letting her hide her emotions from Ronin's sharp scrutiny.

She was afraid to move, to even draw a deep breath, in case it broke the spell that currently bound her. The spell that made her want to believe this could last forever. But she knew that, soon, any thought of forever would be gone, just as the darkness would fade into light as the sun rose on the new day.

He'd be leaving before her this morning. The helicopter was due to collect him at seven thirty to take him to a site near Rotorua for the day. She'd be packed and gone before his return.

A knife twisted in her chest. It was cowardly to sneak away without actually saying goodbye—but she hardened her heart against the shame. She'd leave a note—clichéd, true, but necessary in this case, because if she had to talk to him face-to-face she'd cave and tell him everything. The thought of having to explain her imperfections made her feel sick. No, she'd let herself take the coward's way out this time. She'd save her energy and her determination to face the days ahead. It was time to gather what was left of her strength around her like a carapace. To go on as she'd gone on before. Although this time she knew it would be more difficult than anything she'd ever done.

Ronin's alarm discreetly buzzed, and he flung out an arm to turn it off. Ali feigned sleep as he eased from their embrace and left the bed. She sensed him looking at her, but she focused on keeping her breathing even, her limbs relaxed. Words were useless to her right now, and the last thing she wanted to do was to meet his gaze. People always said that eyes were the window to the soul—if he looked into hers right now she doubted she could hide the sorrow and regret that lingered there.

When he left the room, she felt his absence like a physical pain. *Get used to it,* she told herself, burrowing her face into her pillow. *It's going to get a whole lot worse before it gets better. If it gets better.*

Twenty minutes later, a whiff of his cologne mingled with the fresh scent of mint as he leaned over her and pressed his lips to her shoulder. She mumbled something indistinct and felt him pull away. In the distance she could hear the whup-whup-whup of the helicopter rotors as it approached the house.

Please go, she chanted silently. *Please go so I don't have to say goodbye out loud.*

She heard a faint sigh, and felt the briefest touch on her back. Then he was gone. Only minutes later the helicopter departed.

Ali forced herself from the bed and to the wardrobe, where she'd stored her suitcase and her things. Packing didn't take long. She took a quick shower, dressed in a suit for work and automatically applied her makeup. Her hair was a tangled chaotic mess that she lacked the energy to fix, so she twisted it into a chignon of sorts and viciously pinned it into place.

Taking her case downstairs and putting it in her car only took a couple of minutes, which left just one more thing for Ali to do before she left the house. No, she corrected herself, two things. She had to say goodbye to Joshua and she had to write Ronin a note of farewell.

Right now she didn't know which was the lesser of two evils, and it wasn't like she could rock/paper/scissors with herself. What the hell, she thought, she was downstairs already. She'd write the note in Ronin's office and leave it on the kitchen table for when he returned. Then she'd find the courage she needed to say goodbye to the tiny human who had completely captured her heart and now held it hostage in his perfect little hands.

Choosing the right words to say to Ronin was more difficult than she'd expected, even though she'd had several hours to think about it. In the end, she kept the note short and sweet, thanking him for giving her the opportunity to create Joshua's nursery and for opening his home to her. She finished by saying she'd never forget him, but that in the long term she felt it was better if they parted. No reason. No excessive explanation. Before she could change her mind she shoved it into an envelope, sealed it and wrote his name across the front.

Once she'd put it on the kitchen table, she made herself return up the stairs to the nursery. She could hear Joshua already, his cries mingling with the nanny's soothing tones.

"Good morning," Ali said, forcing a smile to her face as she entered the nursery. "Someone sounds grumpy this morning."

"Nothing his morning bottle won't fix," the nanny said serenely as she changed Joshua's diaper and then lifted him from the changing table. "Would you like to hold him while I get his bottle?"

"I'd love to, and if you don't mind, I'll give him his bottle, too."

It would be the last time, she told herself. The very last.

"No problem. I'll be back in a moment." The nanny smiled, handing the baby into Ali's willing arms and leaving the nursery.

Ali cuddled Joshua close, but instead of settling as he usually did, he continued to cry. She studied his wrinkled face and tried to soothe him, but to no avail. Did he sense her unhappiness? she wondered, feeling her own tears prickling near the surface as his wails picked up in volume.

She tried to find any sign of her ex-husband in the baby's features—any reason, no matter how inane, not to feel this overwhelming love for the infant in her arms. She failed completely. Whether he'd grow to look like Richard, or his wife, or whether he'd be his own little person, it didn't matter. She loved him wholly from top to toe. Even so, she had to walk away.

"Hush, little man. Hush," she whispered, lifting him to her shoulder and rocking from side to side. "How can I say goodbye when you won't let me get a word in?"

She kissed the top of his little head and inhaled his sweet baby scent, knowing this had been a bad idea. She should simply have left. Why had she been determined to prolong the agony? Joshie was more than well cared for. He didn't need her anymore. And he certainly wouldn't know one way or another if she said goodbye.

The nanny came back into the room, bottle in hand.

"Here you are," she said, offering the bottle to Ali.

"I've just remembered I have an early appointment at the office. Do you mind terribly if I leave you to it?"

It was the coward's way out again, she knew, but right now it was the only thing she could manage to do. If she didn't leave this minute, she might never find the courage to go—at least until, maybe, she was forced to. And she couldn't bear that again. Far better to pre-empt it now than to open herself up for an even greater world of hurt.

"Not at all," the nanny said, with one of her calming smiles.

Ali gave Joshie one last kiss and passed him back to the nanny, then compelled her lips into a smile.

"I've left a note downstairs for Mr. Marshall. Could you see that he gets it?"

"Sure. I'm going off shift shortly but I'll make sure the new nanny coming on lets him know."

"That's great, thanks. Well, I'd better be off."

Despite her undeniable need to leave, to get away and put some distance between here and getting her life back together, she found herself reluctant to go.

"Have a nice day, Ms. Carter," the nanny said, offering the bottle to her charge and turning away.

She couldn't bring herself to answer. Nice days would be a thing of the past for quite a while. Possibly even forever. She waved a hand in response, and ignoring the crushing weight that built in her chest, went down the stairs and to her car. Her hand shook uncontrollably as she tried to put her key in the ignition and she forced herself to take several deep breaths before trying again.

"You can do this," she said out loud. "It's not the end of the world."

No, it might not be the end of the world, her inner voice reminded her. But it was the end of hope as she knew it.

As she headed down the long driveway she didn't look back. She had a busy day ahead, with no time to dwell on "might have beens" or "if onlys." She'd already had a bellyful of them the first time around. And she'd learned her lesson this time, at least. It didn't pay to fall in love. It only set you up for immeasurable loss.

Storming through the front entrance of Best for Baby felt more than a little like déjà vu, Ronin thought, and he had just about the same head of steam built up this time, too. A problem at the project yesterday, followed by a delay with the helicopter that had eventually seen him hire a car to drive home from Rotorua, had made him very late home last night. Too late to do anything about the ridiculous note he'd found waiting for him on the kitchen table when he'd finally gotten home, or the empty bed he'd been forced to toss and turn in.

Yesterday had been a crock from start to finish. He rubbed a hand across eyes that still felt scratchy from lack of sleep and looked around the reception area. Just like the last time, there was no one in attendance. He reached for the bell on the countertop just as Deb came through from what he assumed was a kitchenette, judging by the tray of coffee cups she carried.

"Oh!" she cried when she saw him, the cups rattling a little as she startled.

"Is Ali in? I need to see her."

"She's not expecting you," Deb stated firmly, as if that would be enough to make him turn tail and leave.

Ronin studied the other woman carefully. Did she really think she could stop him from seeing Ali if that's what he wanted to do? Something of his determination must have shown on his face, because she put the tray down on her desk and stepped in front of him, barring his access to Ali's door.

"Is she in her office?" he asked.

Deb's body language gave him all the response he needed.

"She's with clients and can't be disturbed," Deb replied implacably. "Look, now really isn't a good time."

Ronin cast a look at the tray Deb had been carrying. Yes, there were three cups and saucers there and a small plate of bite-sized servings of what looked like chocolate-and-caramel slice.

"I'll wait," he replied, settling himself on one of the two-seater sofas in the waiting area.

"Mr. Marsh—" Deb started, but he cut her off.

"I said, I'll wait."

He reached for the morning paper, still folded neatly on the coffee table in front of him, and, crossing his legs, began to read. Deb threw him a fulminating look. Clearly she knew that Ali had left him, and had been prepared to run interference, but she was no match for his purpose. He watched from behind the paper as she sniffed in his direction then picked up the tray and knocked on Ali's office door before going in. As she closed the door carefully behind her, he caught a glimpse of a couple seated opposite Ali's desk.

So, she had a consultation. It shouldn't take more than an hour, tops, surely. He settled himself more comfortably on the sofa, quite prepared to wait her out. The printed ink on the sheets in his hands blurred before his eyes as his mind wandered.

He'd known there was something up with Ali on Sunday night. Even when they'd made love, she'd been different. Although she'd been no less involved in what they were doing than usual, there'd been a degree of desperation about her he'd found hard to define. For the life of him he couldn't understand why, or even *when*, things had changed. Everything had been going so well. They'd been happy, hadn't they? So what the hell had gone so terribly wrong?

His phone buzzed in his pocket and he checked the screen, diverting the incoming call to his voice mail. There was only one matter he was prepared to deal with right now, and that involved the person sitting in the office on the other side of that wall.

Deb came out of Ali's office and closed the door behind her again, then flung him another look that told him in no uncertain terms that she wasn't happy about him being there. Well, she could be unhappy about it. This was too important for him to be ruffled by her behavior.

It was coming up on forty minutes when he heard Ali's door open again, followed by her voice thanking the couple for choosing Best for Baby. He knew the precise moment she realized he was here. Her face suddenly paled, and the smile that had been on her face disappeared. She appeared to quickly gather herself together, but he discerned a faint tremor in the hand she offered her clients as she said goodbye.

"I'll leave Deb to get your full contact details and we'll forward you a proposal for your baby's nursery by the end of the week. Have a great rest of your day," Ali said to the glowingly pregnant woman and her slightly distracted-looking husband.

Ronin waited to see what she'd do next. He expected her to come toward him, but instead she turned on her very high heel and went back into her office. Before she could shut the door, he was there.

"You don't want me to make a scene in front of your new clients, do you?" he said, his voice pitched only for her hearing.

For a second he swore she was considering it, but then she held the door wide and said, "Come in." As she closed it, she continued, "This had better be quick. I have an onsite appointment I need to head out to very shortly."

He studied her carefully, noting the strain around her eyes and the continued lack of color in her cheeks. Quick? She wanted quick? He wasn't going anywhere until this was sorted out. Fury and frustration vied for equal dominance as he shoved his hand in his suit pocket and dragged out her note. He held it up between them.

"*This* was your idea of saying goodbye?" he demanded. "I think we both know I deserved more than that."

"Not used to being turned down?" she answered glibly, moving behind her desk as if the expanse of wood and paper could protect her from his questions.

"It has nothing to do with that and you know it," he persisted. "You don't spend a night together like we had and then simply up and leave the next morning with this pathetic piece of—"

"Please," she hissed, interrupting him before he could tell her what he really thought of her note. "Keep your voice down."

"Then tell me why, Ali? Why did you leave?"

"Look, isn't it enough for me to say that I feel we can't see each other anymore? We rushed into things. It was all just too much."

Too much? It had felt just right to him, and he'd have wagered his very substantial salary that it had felt pretty damn good to her, too. Confusion over her choice of words clouded his thoughts, feeding the anger and frustration that had been building in him since he'd read her short, cold note. He didn't like feeling this way. It was foreign to him. He fixed things. He was organized and logical. He liked life clear-cut, and this was anything but.

The only thing Ronin knew for certain was that he wanted her back. It was the solution to a problem he couldn't even fully define. From the day he met Ali he'd been acting out of character. He'd reached for things with her that he'd never dreamed of sharing with anyone else. But even acting out of character had felt right, with her.

She'd literally rocked his world and made it a better place after everything around him had gone to hell in a handbasket. Mentally, he'd committed to her. Physically, he'd committed to her. Surely she could see that.

When he remained silent, fighting with the thoughts that swirled uncharacteristically in his normally linear mind, she continued.

"Ronin, I have an appointment. I have to go. Please respect my wishes. I don't want to see you again."

Her lips had moved and the words had come out, but he remained unconvinced that she meant them. It was time to regroup, he decided, to give her some space and sort out his next steps. He needed to get his own head straight rather than going off at her half-cocked.

"This isn't over yet, Ali," he said as he turned to leave.

"It has to be," she answered, a quaver in her voice.

He couldn't bring himself to reply, but he did as she'd bade him and left her office. Ignoring Deb, who jumped from her seat as if she'd been given an electric shock, he exited the offices. All the while, he felt himself forming a new resolve. He'd get to the bottom of what had scared her away. It was what he did. He had always solved the most intricate of problems, eventually.

And he would again, because—in this matter, even more than anything else he'd achieved in his life to date—failure was simply not an option.

Fourteen

Ali headed for home with a heavy heart. This week had been a tough one. It had been busy, which was fantastic for business, but it had been lonely, too. Every aspect of her job had her dealing with happy couples, who just reminded her every day of what she'd walked away from with Ronin. Now, it was Friday evening and she had an entire empty weekend to look forward to. She couldn't even visit family, as her sisters and their husbands and children had headed away on a Pacific Island cruise with her parents.

She had, of course, been invited to join them on the cruise, but she'd had to decline. She'd already booked her non-refundable tickets to Hawaii before her family had found out about the special price promotion, and she couldn't justify the cost of the cruise or the time away from the office when she'd just gotten back from her own holiday. She wished now she'd found some way to make it work to go with them. She'd known their trip was coming up, but she hadn't expected to feel so alone when they left.

Deb, too, had plans for the weekend. A lovely romantic retreat with her husband. An unreasonable pang of envy hit Ali in the stomach. Everyone, it seemed, was happy but her. "Get over yourself," she grumbled aloud as she parked her car and then took the stairs to her second-story apartment. The bottle of wine she had in a grocery bag would go a long way toward making up for company tonight, she decided, along with the magazine, the antipasto selection and the half loaf of French bread she'd picked up at the same time. Tomorrow, and the rest of the weekend? Well, she'd tackle each hour, each minute, as it came.

She began to ferret around in her handbag for her front door key, her head bent and not looking where she was going, when a deep male voice arrested her in her task.

"Can I take those for you?"

Ronin! What was he doing here? Since his visit to her office on Tuesday she'd all but convinced herself that her plea had finally sunk in with him and that he'd accepted she didn't want to see him anymore. Her body called her a liar on that score the instant she lifted her head. His hair was spikier than usual, as if he'd been running his fingers through it repeatedly, and the stubble on his jaw was longer than she was accustomed to seeing. Her skin tingled as she remembered just how it had felt when those whiskers had rasped along her inner thigh or over her breasts.

She slammed the door closed on her wayward thoughts. She'd turned her back on that part of her life. On him. What the hell was he doing here?

"I thought I made myself clear," she said, still juggling her shopping bag in her attempt to find her house key.

In response, Ronin relieved her of her groceries as she finally wrapped her fingers around the missing keychain.

"You did. I'd like to talk. That's all."

Every nerve, every cell in her body tensed at his words. Talk? When had they really just talked? Perhaps the last time had been when they'd had that lunch on Waiheke Island. Before he'd gone to Vietnam. Before Joshie had come home. At the thought of the infant boy her insides twisted sharply. Her arms ached with the need to hold him again—but he wasn't hers to hold, she'd told herself that. Convinced herself she'd get over it. If Ronin would only leave her alone, maybe she'd actually begin to believe it, too.

She sighed. "Fine. Come in, then."

Ali flipped on the overhead light only to have the bulb blow out. Muttering under her breath, she used the light from her cell phone to guide her to the other side of the room, where she flicked on an occasional lamp. With its burnished shade, it cast a warm and cozy glow about the room. Too cozy. All they needed were some candles and, with her wine, the scene would be set for seduction. Except she didn't need to seduce Ronin. Though he was clearly upset with her, she could feel the chemistry between them hadn't diminished one bit. She knew he was hers for the taking if she was willing to put in a little effort, but she didn't want him.

Liar. The voice inside her head slithered from her mind's darkest recesses. The same voice that clearly held sway with the part of her brain that created the dreams that had found her waking, several times each night, wracked with frustration and sorrow combined.

"Can I offer you something to drink?" she forced herself to ask. "Some wine perhaps?"

"Sure, a glass of wine would be nice. Thank you."

He handed her the grocery bag and sat down on a sofa she'd found at a bargain price at the local thrift store. It was comfortable, even if the color, a virulent chartreuse green, was a little hard on the eyes.

Ali busied herself in the kitchen, pouring each of them a glass of the imported Australian Shiraz she'd bought. She eyed the antipasto and French bread. *What the heck,* she thought, and quickly sliced some bread and laid all the ingredients on a long ceramic platter. She had to eat anyway. Might as well be a good hostess at the same time.

She brought the items through to the small sitting room and, once she'd offered him his wine and something to eat, sat down opposite Ronin.

"You said you want to talk," she started. "So talk."

Ronin leaned forward and put his wine on the coffee table untouched. He rested his elbows on his knees and clasped his hands loosely together. Ali waited for him to start, but when he remained silent she felt the atmosphere between them thicken and become awkward. Eventually he spoke.

"I've been trying to make sense of why you left."

"Ronin, we've been through this—"

"No, we haven't. All that's happened is that you wrote a note and said you were leaving, then when I came to see you, you told me you didn't want to see me again. Why?"

Ali closed her eyes and shook her head slightly. She didn't want to go through this. Couldn't he just accept that things were over? People broke up all the time. They moved on. Period. Why wouldn't he let her go?

Maybe because he loves you? The idea came out of the blue. Her lungs squeezed closed and she struggled to draw in a breath. She didn't want him to love her. He couldn't, or at least he wouldn't when he knew she wasn't what he really wanted. But could she bring herself to tell him?

"Ali?" he prompted.

She opened her eyes. "Ronin, sometimes things just don't work out. We have to accept that and move on."

"Don't work out? What part of *us* wasn't working out? Were you unhappy with me, with Joshua? From what I could tell everything was fine until my parents came around on Sunday afternoon. Even then everything was great…" He hesitated a moment, as if working something out in his mind. "Right up until Mum showed you the album. Was that what it was? Was there something in there that upset you?"

Everything in her wanted to tell him to get up and leave right now. She didn't want to discuss this. Didn't want to strip herself totally bare and admit the truth to him. But if she didn't do it now, she realized, he would keep chipping away at her until he unraveled the ball of knots that was her past, her pain.

"Ali, I want to fix this. How can I make it right for you if you won't tell me what's wrong?" he said, more gently than she'd ever heard him speak before.

Oh how she wished it could be that simple. That she could just tell him and have him wipe every slate clean so they could start anew. But over the past few years, she'd learned to be a realist. Some things were simply unfixable. She cupped her wineglass in her hands and took a deep breath.

"It's nothing you can fix. It's me."

"C'mon, Ali. At least give me a chance."

She looked at him, at the intensity and integrity reflected back at her in his eyes. He really believed that he could make a difference? She hated to burst his bubble of confidence. But maybe that was what it would take for him to take that step back and release her to her solitude.

"I guess I should start at the beginning, then," she said with a deep sigh. "I first met Richard, my ex-husband, in high school—we were both sixteen. We were pretty much inseparable right from the start. He was so different to the other guys. He wasn't about the here and now, he always had his future clearly in his sights. Part of that future was to have a big family. He was an only child and his parents were in their forties when he came along. His arrival had come as a bit of a shock, I think. I got the sense that it was a fairly lonely childhood for him, though his parents loved him very much. Anyway, he had a plan already mapped out, even when he was sixteen. He knew exactly what he wanted from life and nothing would deter him from his course."

"He sounds focused," Ronin commented.

"Oh, he was. Very much so. I liked that, especially since our goals were so similar. I'm the youngest of four girls and my older sisters were already marrying and starting families when Richard and I started dating. Being a wife and mother was all I ever wanted, really. I didn't want to be a highflier in business. I wanted to create a world filled with the kind of warmth and love that my parents had given to us girls. The kind of world my sisters were creating with their partners for their families. Anyway, once Richard graduated from university he got work as a business analyst and he was very good at it. We married and started trying for a family straightaway."

Ali paused and took a long sip of her wine. This was harder than she'd thought it would be. Relating the bare bones of what had been both the happiest and the most devastating time of her life without injecting it with the emotions that bubbled so close to the surface was enough to have her heart racing with the strain.

She looked across at Ronin, who had leaned back against the back of the sofa and was watching her carefully, his relaxed pose encouraging her to continue.

"Anyway, long story short, we had trouble conceiving and Richard was frustrated that his plans, *our* plans, had stalled. When we discovered the reason why we were having trouble, he changed. He began to withdraw from me, refusing to talk about what the news meant for us as a couple. I thought he just needed time to get his head around the fact that his grand life plan had to be reevaluated, but that we'd be able to go forward on a new track after that. I thought he loved me enough to see us weather through it all."

Her voice cracked on the last few words, and she struggled to pull herself together. She thought she'd learned to control the hurt and sense of betrayal that had remained as the legacy of her marriage, but hard on the heels of her discovery last Sunday—on seeing that gloriously happy photo of Richard with his new bride—she'd realized any control she'd thought she'd had was merely a front. The hurt still cut like a razor, still made her bleed inside.

She shook her head as if to clear her thoughts and continued. "Anyway, one day he came home from work and said he loved someone else who had made him happy again, and he wanted a divorce. In her he saw a new chance to live his dream, to create the future and the world he wanted more than he wanted me. I was blindsided. God, I was such a fool.

"For months he'd been having an affair with a woman he'd hired to redecorate his offices at work. He'd been falling in love with her and out of love with me. I should have realized. I knew how focused he was, how determined he'd always been to reach his goals. I should have realized that once he saw I couldn't give him what he dreamed of, he'd want out."

Ali looked at Ronin again and could see him processing what she'd told him. She could pinpoint the moment when the pieces fell together to make a whole.

"Richard was R.J.?" he asked.

She nodded. "I had no idea he'd remarried, no idea he'd been about to become a father. I hadn't even heard he was dead."

The thought that he'd been on the verge of realizing his greatest goal in life, only to have it snatched cruelly away, made her feel an ironic sense of loss on his behalf.

"I'm so sorry you had to find out that way. No wonder you weren't yourself after seeing the album. And I think I understand why you were so angry when you thought I was married, but——" he shoved a hand through his hair "——I still don't understand why you ran. We could have talked about this. Yes, the situation is unusual, and I understand if it changes the way you view Joshua and me, but we can hardly be held accountable for what R.J. did. You're feeling hurt now, but once the initial shock has passed, I'm sure we can work through it."

"You don't understand," Ali replied, putting her glass down on the table and twisting her hands together.

"Then tell me, so I can do something about it."

"There's nothing you can do, Ronin. It's not just that

my husband cheated on me with your sister. It's not just that together they created a baby, or even that I ended up looking after that baby when he came home from hospital. None of that really matters now."

"No, you're right. We matter. Working out a solution to what's keeping us apart is what matters most."

"You're not listening to me. There is no solution. Tell me if I'm wrong, but I'm sure that when I came out to see you after Hawaii, you said you'd always imagined filling your house with kids, yes?"

"Y-es," Ronin answered carefully, his gaze not budging from her face for a second.

"And didn't you imply to your mother that you planned to give Joshie brothers and sisters in the future?"

"I did, but I'm not in a hurry for that, Ali. We can wait."

She gritted her teeth. Did she have to spell it out in foot-high letters? "Ronin, you won't ever have that with me. I can't have children. Ever."

His eyes dulled a little, but only for a second. Before she knew it they'd fired up again, deepening and glittering in the soft light of her sitting room.

"We'll have Joshua. That's fine. You love him—I saw it with my own eyes. Surely you don't love him any less now because of who his parents were? We can make this work, trust me. If I have no other children than him, I can live with that."

She swallowed against the lump in her throat and gave a humorless laugh. "*Live with that?* For now, maybe. But what about a year from now, or five years from now? What about when your friends have children? When you see families down at the beach or playing in the park? What then? Can you honestly tell me you won't regret not having had more children of your own?"

His silence gave her all the answer she needed.

"And what about me?" she continued, pressing her advantage. "How do you think I'll feel, seeing those families, knowing I'm the reason you can't have one? How can I feel like anything other than a failure as a woman when I'm often reminded of what I can't give you? When our only child is, quite literally, the son I could never give my husband?"

She stood up from her seat, her legs unstable and weak beneath her. As much as she loved him, there was no way she'd put either of them through the hell that she knew would come. Even if he thought he loved her now, she knew regrets would eventually peel away their affection for one another until all that was left was resentment and reproach.

"I'd like you to leave now," she said, as levelly as she was able.

She walked to the front door and held it open, leaving him no other choice but to go.

When Ronin drew level with her, he stopped. "You've got it all wrong, Ali. We can make this work. I know we can."

"You forget, Ronin. I've been through all of that, and it hurt. In fact it hurt so badly that I'm never going to put myself in that position again."

Fifteen

For the duration of his forty-minute drive back home, Ronin turned over every word Ali had said during their meeting. For the first time in his life he was up against a problem that refused to be solved.

And despite what she seemed to think, her infertility was *not* the problem. So what if she couldn't have children? That wasn't the be-all and end-all of his existence. He loved *her*. Not her ability to procreate, and not her instinctive skill as a mother. Her. The problem was her refusal to believe that she could be enough—that he loved her far more than any vague dreams of having a big family.

He groaned out loud. And had he told her that? Had he reassured her that he didn't just look at her as a baby-making machine? Had he so much as hinted at the fact that even if they didn't have Joshua in their lives that she would be enough for him, for all time?

And he thought that he was so clever. That he was Mr. Organized. That the right decision could always be reached with sound deductive reasoning. There was nothing reasonable about the cards life had dealt to Ali. No clear-cut guidelines existed to show a person how to handle successive blows like that. Life didn't come with a handbook, and after the number that R.J. had done on her it was no wonder she felt so insecure about herself.

A part of him wanted to turn his car around and head straight back to her tiny apartment and make his claim on her heart. To tell her he loved her and that he would make everything all right. But the other part, the logical part that ruled his life and governed his decisions, could see that not even a declaration of love would convince Ali that he meant what he said.

But there had to be something. One way or another, he'd nail down a resolution to her fears. He just had to.

A week later, Ronin walked the hallway between the nursery and his master suite with Joshua on his shoulder. The baby simply would not settle down for his afternoon sleep. He'd been fussy and cranky as all get-out for nearly two weeks now, and had failed to make any significant weight gain since Ali had left. Could it be that he missed her as much as Ronin did? Or was this just one of so many different facets of raising a child?

"Would you like me to take him, Mr. Marshall?" the day nanny asked as she came upstairs with a bundle of Joshie's laundry.

It was remarkable the amount of work one tiny baby created, Ronin thought. He wondered anew how single parents who couldn't afford professional childcare coped with the responsibility and the workload. With the doubts about whether you were doing the right thing, and the fears of what might happen if you didn't. It reminded him that he hadn't shown Ali anywhere near sufficient appreciation for what she'd done caring for the fretting child in his arms on her own, as she had when he'd first gotten out of the hospital.

"It's okay," Ronin replied. "He'll settle, eventually."

He didn't want to simply hand Joshua off to the nearest set of willing hands. He'd taken his sister's baby on with all that had entailed. And if that meant walking him up and down this hallway until he wore a track in the carpet, then that's exactly what he'd do. It wasn't easy, though, and a man could go deaf with the noise reverberating in his ear.

Ronin took his guardianship seriously, as he did any project he accepted. Except this was different in so many ways. He'd never been as emotionally invested in his work projects as he was in this tiny individual. And while he loved his work, it certainly didn't hold a candle to how he'd felt when, a couple of days ago, Joshie had beamed a gummy smile in his direction.

But the baby wasn't smiling now. Another ten minutes felt like sixty. Ronin was suddenly reminded of how quickly Joshua had settled when he'd held him in the hospital. What had they called it again? Kangaroo cuddles. Anything was worth a shot. He went into the nursery and put Joshua on the change table while he quickly pulled off his T-shirt, then eased the baby's onesie off as well. Clad only in his jeans and with Joshie in just a diaper, he sat down in the rocker and slung a blanket around them both to keep them warm.

The baby headbutted him a few times, still voicing his discontent, but as Ronin set the chair to move gently back and forth, Joshie finally calmed and dropped off to sleep. Ronin's first instinct was to put the baby back in his bassinet and leave him to it, but as he looked down at his nephew a new sense of wonderment stole over him. He'd forgotten how special it felt to hold the baby to his heart. To feel his little sigh of release as he let go of wakefulness and slid into slumber.

Only six weeks old and Joshua had already changed so much from the helpless scrap Ronin had first seen in the newborn intensive care unit. Ronin wasn't the kind of man who gave his heart easily, but when he did, he went all the way, and he knew without doubt that he'd cross shark-infested waters if Joshua needed him on the other side. He'd do anything to protect Joshie—to make sure he was safe and happy.

So what did that really mean? What would it take to give Joshie the life that he deserved? Ronin had been convinced that the rotation of nannies would be enough to see to the baby's care, freeing him up to lend a hand when possible and mostly just oversee it all. But the past two weeks had proven that that wasn't enough. Joshie needed something more—something that Ronin seemingly couldn't give the baby, no matter how much he loved him. In fact, it was *because* he loved his nephew so much that he had to come to terms with the truth.

He'd followed his sister's wishes by stepping up to raise her son, but had he really done what was best? Was his certainty that he could handle the challenges of being a parent well-founded, or was it just arrogant? Was he overconfident in his abilities to complete any task he laid out for himself? Had his pride, and his certainty in his own abilities, blinded him to what the baby really needed?

He thought back to CeeCee and R.J.'s funeral, to his cousin Julia's offer to take the baby and raise him with her family. Should he have done that? Given Joshie a mum and a dad? Would it have been the best thing for Joshie in the long run? He couldn't say one way or the other, but he knew it was an idea he'd have to seriously consider. Joshie's future was at stake, and he couldn't afford to make the wrong choice. Nor would he forgive himself if he denied the baby the chance to have a loving mother's care—care that he was obviously missing since Ali had left.

But as he weighed his decision over in his mind another thought butted in from left field. He turned the idea this way and that, examining it from all angles. It would be risky, he thought, and he couldn't go at it halfheartedly—it was something to which he had to be prepared to commit fully. Could he do it?

He looked down at the sleeping baby nestled against him. Love and devotion filled him in equal proportion. Of course he could do it if he had to, no matter how much it contradicted his every instinct to hold on. He'd do whatever was best for Joshua, always.

Carefully, Ronin rose from the rocker and tucked the baby into his bassinet, making sure his bedcovers were snugly tucked around him. Ronin tugged his shirt back on and exited the nursery, bumping into the day nanny as he did so.

"Success?" she said softly, with a conspiratorial smile.

"Yes. It was a bit of a battle of wills, but we got there in the end."

"He's lucky to have you."

"I think I'm lucky to have him," Ronin replied before making his way downstairs to his office.

He *was* lucky to have Joshua, which made what he was about to do all the more important. And he had to do it right—for everyone's sakes.

* * *

By Monday morning everything was in place. Ronin secured Joshua in his car seat in the car and headed toward Best for Baby. Joshua, thankfully, slept through the morning rush hour traffic that kept them bound in gridlock on the Southern Motorway, stirring only briefly when Ronin pulled into the visitor parking at Ali's office. He didn't see her car there, which promised a potential wrinkle in his plans, but he knew he wouldn't be that easily deterred. He'd find out when she was due in and adjust accordingly.

With the car seat hooked over his arm, he entered the office. Deb looked up from the reception desk with a smile as he pushed open the doors. A smile that froze, then faded, as she recognized him.

"Can I help you?" she asked, in an arctic tone.

"I'd like to see Ali. It's important."

"She's not here. In fact, I don't expect her in all day."

The woman looked uncomfortable, almost pitying, as she imparted the information.

"As I said, it's important." He hefted Joshie's carrier onto the reception desk and saw Deb's eyes soften as she looked upon his, currently, angelic face.

"He's doing well, now, is he?" she asked, looking up briefly at Ronin.

"Not so great these past couple of weeks. Neither of us are."

She got his point immediately.

"He misses Ali?"

"I've taken him to his pediatrician and she confirmed there's nothing physically wrong with him, so yes, I believe so."

Deb reached out, and with the back of one finger stroked Joshua's round little cheek.

"It's a crime that she can't have babies, you know that."

"It is," he agreed vehemently.

"But the worst crime is the way it makes her feel about herself—as if she doesn't hold value as a woman without the ability to bear children. I don't want to speak ill of the dead, but Richard crushed her sense of self-worth when he left the way that he did. For a while her family and I didn't expect her to recover, but after the divorce was finalized, she rallied. That's when she poured everything she had into this place. All her longing, all her love, it goes into every contract we make, every family she helps."

Ronin didn't speak—a tactic he'd learned many years ago that usually led him to exactly the information he wanted. Most people were uncomfortable with a vacuum of silence. It appeared Deb was no different from the rest.

"If I tell you where she is, will you promise not to hurt her? If you do, I *will* have to hurt you."

He looked at the diminutive figure seated behind the reception desk. Based on her build he doubted the woman could hurt a fly, but given the look in her eyes, Ronin chose his words carefully. "It isn't, and has never been, my intention to hurt her."

Deb gave him a hard look. "I'd like to ask you your intentions, but I have a feeling you'd probably tell me they're none of my business."

He couldn't help it—he smiled at her perceptiveness. "You're probably right."

She smiled in return and grabbed a small sheet of paper, on which she scrawled an address.

"The tenant above her had a water leak and it flooded Ali's apartment. She's staying a few nights at her par-

ents' house while her landlord makes the necessary re-
pairs and dries her place out. She's working from there
today. And her family's away, just in case you were
wondering."

"Thank you," he said, studying the address and then
slipping the paper into his pocket.

Knowing her parents weren't around was a relief.
While he was prepared to do this with an audience if
he had to, he vastly preferred to keep this just between
the three of them.

"Mr. Marshall, I meant what I said about hurting
her."

"And I meant what I said, too."

She nodded, accepting that would have to suffice.

"As long as we're clear on that."

"Crystal," he replied, reaching for the carrier.

As he neared the door, Deb caught his attention once
more.

"Mr. Marshall?"

He turned around.

"For what it's worth, she's missed you, too. Both of
you. Good luck."

He smiled in response. He needed all the luck he
could get. Everything hinged on this going as he'd
hoped. Everything.

Ali's parents' house was a simple weatherboard bungalow in one of the older parts of town. A bed of tired-
looking standard roses stood in a circular garden in the
middle of the front lawn. He walked up the narrow con-
crete front path with a now wide-awake Joshua in the
car seat. The baby startled when Ronin rapped on the
multipaned rippled glass front door, but he didn't cry.

Ronin spied Ali coming up a hallway toward the

door. She hesitated when she figured out it was him, but then she eventually lifted an arm and warily opened the door.

"What do I have to say to you, Ronin? I told you I don't want to see you anymore."

Dressed simply in jeans and a long-sleeved T-shirt, she'd never looked so appealing. His hands itched to reach out and touch her. To trace the signs of tiredness that were drawn on her face. To kiss the firm set of her lips into a softer, more welcoming state. He swallowed and drew in a breath. This wasn't going to be easy, but then again, he certainly didn't expect it to be.

"I thought you might like to say goodbye to Joshua before he leaves."

She paled, her gaze flicking from the baby to him. "L-leaves? Why?"

He used the silence tactic, determinedly holding her gaze.

Ali sighed and opened the door a little wider. "You'd better come in."

She led him into a simply furnished sitting room. He looked around, seeing the everyday things that made up a family's life. The photos on the display cabinet, the clumsy school project crafts and sculptures that took pride of place within it, peppered in between fine china cups and saucers that probably never so much as saw a drop of tea or a cookie unless "company" came to visit. He put Joshua's carrier on a floral-covered couch and stepped over to look at the photo frames on the cabinet.

So many of them, he thought, and all of them family. He picked Ali out immediately in a picture of four little girls, arrayed from left to right, oldest to youngest. He felt his heart tug. She'd grown up surrounded by family. A family that had expanded as her sisters, who he recognized in newer photos, had children of their own. He felt a jolt of shock as he recognized R.J. in a frame shoved to the back—or, more particularly, R.J. and Ali on their wedding day.

Her dress was simple and she had such a look of optimism and devotion on her face as she looked up at her new husband. So much hope, so many dreams. Could Ronin even begin to hope that one day he might see that look on her face when it was turned to him? There was only one way to find out.

"Well?" Ali demanded from behind him. "What did you mean about Joshua leaving?"

He turned to face her, noting how her regard kept drifting toward Joshie, recognized the longing there. Despite what he'd told Deb, he knew what he was about to say was going to hurt. But sometimes, he knew, you had to be cruel to be kind. You just had to rip the bandage off in one hard swipe to allow true healing to begin.

"I'm giving him up."

Sixteen

"W-what?" He had her full attention now. "What do you mean you're giving him up? You're his guardian. You can't just *give him up!*"

"I mean I can't do it—I can't raise him on my own. He deserves more than I can give him. I've tried and I've looked at this from every angle. Yes, I can look after his basic needs. He's fed and cared for, he's got shelter and, yes, he's loved. But I know what my sister wanted for him—what any parent wants for their child, and what Joshie himself has been suffering without. He deserves people who are totally invested in him. He deserves a complete family—a mother and a father. Even with his rotation of nannies, I can't do that on my own."

"But you do love him, don't you?"

"Of course I love him. But this isn't about me. It's about him, and that's why I have to do what's right by Joshua."

"So, what? You're just going to put him up for adoption? Just like that? What if they're not right for him? What if they don't love him like you do?"

Ronin began to feel something ease a little inside him. She was fighting. Fighting for Joshie. It was a start.

"I'm not letting him go to just anyone. A cousin of mine offered to raise him when CeeCee died. Julia and her husband already have a couple of kids and they want him. Really want him. It's a win-win. He'll stay in the family, and my parents will still have full access to him. Even better, he'll be with people who love him and who will care for him."

"How can you say it's a win-win when you're letting him go?" she asked in confusion. "You're not winning. I don't understand how you can do that…how you can say it's what's best for him. I've seen you with Joshie. I've seen how much you love him. He deserves to stay with you. It's what your sister and—" she paused and took a shuddering breath "—Richard wanted."

Ronin shoved his hands in his trouser pockets and fought to find the right words.

"When they made their wills, I'm sure they didn't expect me to ever actually have to take responsibility for their child or children."

"No one intends to die, but people make contingency plans. They named you as their preferred guardian. You were their first choice. Surely if they wanted your cousin to raise Joshie they'd have mentioned her in their wills."

Ronin's fingers ached, his fists were so tight. It hurt to say this, but he had to.

"And I'm equally sure they always imagined that one day I'd be married and have someone at my side to help me. To love and raise Joshua with me."

"And you will, one day."

He shook his head. "No, I won't."

She looked at him incredulously. "Don't be ridiculous. Of course you will. Let's face it, you're highly eligible."

"Thank you," he acceded wryly. "But eligibility aside, I am not marrying. Not when I can't be with the only woman I want."

Ali backed up until the back of her legs hit the chair behind her. "I beg your pardon?" she said, her voice small and baffled.

"Ali, if I can't have you, I don't want anybody else. You seem to have this misguided notion that I'd want something more than you, or that I'm going to change my mind about my feelings for you. That my first priority is to have more children in my life. It's not. Sure, if you agreed to be with me, and you wanted more kids, I'd be happy to look into adoption. God knows we have the capacity for more kids and more love in the house. But it's not something that's vital to me. You are. Without you, children aren't in the picture anyway, because I won't have them with anyone else. And I won't have Joshie, either, because he deserves to have a loving mother, and the only one I want filling that role in my home is you."

"You can't be serious," she gasped.

"I've never been more serious about anything in my life. I'm not the kind of guy to say things I don't mean, and I'm not the kind of guy who pretends to feel things I don't feel. I've got to do what's right for me—and that means being with you or being alone. If I'm alone, then I can't be the right parent for Joshie. I'm not denying this is going to hurt. It's going to kill me inside. But I can't do everything, or be everyone, that Joshua needs. I have to do what's right for *him*." He paused. "And what's right for *you*. And I can't help thinking that nothing could be better for you than to be with the man who wants to devote his life to making you happy. I love you, Ali, completely, utterly and totally, with everything I am."

Ali stared at him in disbelief then shook her head as if she could shake free the things he'd just said. "It's easy for you to say that now. But I know you'll regret it."

"The only thing I'll ever regret is not being able to convince you that what I'm saying is true."

"You don't want me, Ronin. You couldn't possibly."

All the pain of the past five years swelled within her. All her feelings of inadequacy, and lack of self-worth. She was flawed, incomplete. A reject.

"I'm not Richard. Can't you understand that? I'm not going to stop loving you just because you can't have a baby. That's not why I want to be with you. I'd rather have a childless life than an eternity without you."

"How can you love me?" she cried. "We've known each other just over six weeks. People don't make plans for the rest of their lives based on that."

Even as she said the words she argued with herself. She and Richard had known each other nearly six years when they'd married, but it hadn't changed the outcome. Love didn't have any sort of set time line, and there were no guarantees. She couldn't have known that Richard wouldn't love her forever…but where his love had failed, Ronin's might last. Maybe. Possibly. Could Ronin be telling her the truth? Did he really love her so much that he was prepared to ignore the life he'd always imagined for a life with her? She wanted to believe it was possible, that she was worthy of such a love, but it went against everything she felt, everything she'd learned, when her marriage had folded into nothing.

"Do you love me?" he demanded, breaking into her thoughts.

She lifted her face to meet his gaze. What she saw reflected back at her made the words clogging her throat so much easier to say.

"Of course I love you," she whispered, barely able to let the truth out. Doing so made her vulnerable, opened her to more harm. But at her words, she could see the tension begin to ease from his face, his body.

"Then know this," Ronin replied earnestly. "I'm not normally the kind of man who rushes into things. The only time in my life I have ever done so was with you. But one thing remains constant for me. When I commit to something, or someone, I follow through—all the way. I want to commit to you, Ali, for a lifetime if you'll let me. I won't lie to you. What you see is what you get. I'm not perfect. I can be overly analytical and set in my ways, and I don't embrace change easily, but I want you in my life. Every day. Every night. Forever, if you'll have me."

"What about Joshua?" she asked.

Ronin looked at the little boy who sat, uncharacteristically quiet for a change, in his car seat. Grief struck him anew. For Joshua, for his dead parents and for the sacrifice he was prepared to make to win Ali back.

"He's Richard's son and always will be. I know how much that must distress you. I fully understand if you can't raise Joshua with me. He'll have a good home, I promise you. I won't deny that I'll miss him, but I *will* let him go if it means having you back, Ali. I don't want you to hurt anymore."

Ali looked from him to the baby and back again. She hardly dared to believe his words, but his actions bore him out. He was willing to give up Joshua, despite his love for him, to ensure that both she and Joshua could have happy lives. She couldn't let him do it.

"No," Ali replied shakily.

The tension that had painted his face into stark lines before was back, this time even worse.

"No?" he repeated, his voice hoarse.

"You can't let him go."

That much was patently clear. He loved Joshua as if he were his own child. She'd seen that with her very own eyes. With the baby's parents gone, no one else would, or could, be a better dad for him than Ronin. Ali could see the struggle he went through to hold on to his normally formidable control as her words began to sink in.

"I can't?" His voice was flat, devoid of emotion.

Ali took a deep breath, and then another. She had to make a decision, to either take a leap of faith or to become a victim of all the suffering that had defined her life since Richard had walked out on her. Ronin was offering her a future. One filled with love, with passion, with a family. It was all she'd ever wanted and yet it remained a terrifying prospect. Was she brave enough, woman enough, to take that leap?

"You can't let him go, because I couldn't come to you unless you included Joshie, as well. I love you both too much to lose either one of you again."

Ronin's features lightened. "You won't regret it, Ali. Every day I'll make sure you won't regret it."

"I know," she answered simply.

"Then what are you doing standing over there when you could be here?" he said, opening his arms.

She flew across the room and buried her face in his chest, relishing the sensation of his arms closing around her—holding her safe within the love and assurance he offered. He squeezed her close and a tremor rocked through him, as if he was afraid that if he let go, she'd leave. It made her realize that she hadn't stopped once to consider his feelings in all of this. She'd left him with no real explanation, and when he'd come after her she'd turned him away more than once. All because she'd been too afraid to love again. Too afraid to trust again.

Both concepts still terrified her, she admitted, but deep down she knew that Ronin would help her through her fears. The last couple of weeks without him had been miserable, and she'd mourned both him and little Joshie with an ache that had been as much physical as it was emotional.

"You had me worried there for a while," Ronin admitted. "More than worried. I thought I was happy with my life until you came into it. I enjoyed—no, relished— my rather solitary existence and the challenges of my work. I leapt at the opportunity to troubleshoot problems that arose all over the world, and had the greatest sense of fulfillment when the job was done. But nothing, absolutely nothing, has matched the satisfaction I feel when I'm with you."

She squeezed him tight, the lump in her throat not allowing her to speak.

He continued. "I never realized it was possible to open up to another person without weakening or diminishing myself. I had no idea how loving someone as much as I love you would enrich me—how much it would strengthen me. I never knew, until I met you, that a vital piece was missing from my life."

Any last vestige of doubt that Ali might have harbored disappeared as he spoke, and when he cupped her face and tilted it upward she willingly met his lips, kissing him with a fierceness that told of her love for him, of her need and her desire to never let go of him again.

He lifted his head. "You complete me, Ali Carter. Will you marry me and adopt Joshie with me so we can create our family and our future together?"

"I would be honored to," she said, through happy tears that coursed unchecked down her cheeks. "I love you with all my heart, and I can't believe I could be so lucky as to have you in my life. Both of you."

And as Ronin kissed her again she realized that finally she had everything she ever wanted. A man who loved her unreservedly, and a family to fill her heart for a lifetime.

* * * * *

If you liked THE CHILD THEY DIDN'T EXPECT,
check out Yvonne's other
BILLIONAIRES & BABIES *story!*
A FATHER'S SECRET
Available now from Harlequin Desire!
If you liked this BILLIONAIRE'S & BABIES *novel,*
watch for the next book
in this #1 bestselling Desire series,
The Cowboy's Pride and Joy by
USA TODAY bestselling author Maureen Child,
available November 2014.

COMING NEXT MONTH FROM

HARLEQUIN *Desire*

Available November 4, 2014

#2335 THE COWBOY'S PRIDE AND JOY
Billionaires and Babies • by Maureen Child
A wealthy rancher who loves his reclusive mountain, Jake never could resist Cassidy. Especially not when she introduces him to his infant son...just as a snowstorm forces them to face everything that's still between them...

#2336 SHELTERED BY THE MILLIONAIRE
Texas Cattleman's Club: After the Storm • by Catherine Mann
An unexpected passion ignites between single mom and conservationist Megan and her adversarial neighbor. But when she learns the real estate magnate threatens what she's trying to protect, she has to decide—trust the facts...or her heart?

#2337 FROM ENEMY'S DAUGHTER TO EXPECTANT BRIDE
The Billionaires of Black Castle • by Olivia Gates
Rafael Salazar is poised to destroy the man who stole his childhood, but his feelings for his enemy's daughter may threaten his plans. When she becomes pregnant, will he have to choose between revenge and love?

#2338 A BEAUMONT CHRISTMAS WEDDING
The Beaumont Heirs • by Sarah M. Anderson
As best man and a PR specialist, Matthew Beaumont needs his brother's Christmas wedding to be perfect. Then former wild child Whitney Maddox becomes a bridesmaid. Will she ruin the wedding? Or will Matthew discover the real woman behind the celebrity facade?

#2339 THE BOSS'S MISTLETOE MANEUVERS
by Linda Thomas-Sundstrom
Chad goes undercover at the agency he bought to oversee a Christmas campaign. But when the star ad exec with a strange aversion to the holiday jeopardizes the project, Chad doesn't know whether to fire her or seduce her!

#2340 HER DESERT KNIGHT
by Jennifer Lewis
The last thing Dani needs after her divorce is an affair with a man from the family that's been feuding with hers for decades. But notorious seducer Quasar may be the only man who can reawaken her body...and her heart.

REQUEST YOUR FREE BOOKS!
2 FREE NOVELS PLUS 2 FREE GIFTS!

HARLEQUIN®

Desire

ALWAYS POWERFUL, PASSIONATE AND PROVOCATIVE

YES! Please send me 2 FREE Harlequin Desire® novels and my 2 FREE gifts (gifts are worth about $10). After receiving them, if I don't wish to receive any more books, I can return the shipping statement marked "cancel." If I don't cancel, I will receive 6 brand-new novels every month and be billed just $4.55 per book in the U.S. or $4.99 per book in Canada. That's a savings of at least 13% off the cover price! It's quite a bargain! Shipping and handling is just 50¢ per book in the U.S. and 75¢ per book in Canada.* I understand that accepting the 2 free books and gifts places me under no obligation to buy anything. I can always return a shipment and cancel at any time. Even if I never buy another book, the two free books and gifts are mine to keep forever.

225/326 HDN F4ZC

Name	(PLEASE PRINT)

Address	Apt. #

City	State/Prov.	Zip/Postal Code

Signature (if under 18, a parent or guardian must sign)

Mail to the **Harlequin® Reader Service:**
IN U.S.A.: P.O. Box 1867, Buffalo, NY 14240-1867
IN CANADA: P.O. Box 609, Fort Erie, Ontario L2A 5X3

Want to try two free books from another line?
Call 1-800-873-8635 or visit www.ReaderService.com.

* Terms and prices subject to change without notice. Prices do not include applicable taxes. Sales tax applicable in N.Y. Canadian residents will be charged applicable taxes. Offer not valid in Quebec. This offer is limited to one order per household. Not valid for current subscribers to Harlequin Desire books. All orders subject to credit approval. Credit or debit balances in a customer's account(s) may be offset by any other outstanding balance owed by or to the customer. Please allow 4 to 6 weeks for delivery. Offer available while quantities last.

Your Privacy—The Harlequin® Reader Service is committed to protecting your privacy. Our Privacy Policy is available online at www.ReaderService.com or upon request from the Harlequin Reader Service.

We make a portion of our mailing list available to reputable third parties that offer products we believe may interest you. If you prefer that we not exchange your name with third parties, or if you wish to clarify or modify your communication preferences, please visit us at www.ReaderService.com/consumerschoice or write to us at Harlequin Reader Service Preference Service, P.O. Box 9062, Buffalo, NY 14269. Include your complete name and address.

HD13R

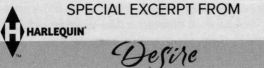
Here's a sneak peek at the next scandalous Beaumont
Heirs book,

A BEAUMONT CHRISTMAS WEDDING
By Sarah M. Anderson

Available November 2014 from Harlequin® Desire.

What if Matthew Beaumont could look at her without caring about who she'd been in the past?

What if—what if he wasn't involved with anyone?

Whitney didn't hook up. That part of her life was dead and buried. But…a little Christmas romance between the maid of honor and the best man wouldn't be such a bad thing, would it? It could be fun.

She hurried to the bathroom, daring to hope that Matthew was single. He was coming to dinner tonight and it sounded as if he would be involved with a lot of the wedding activities.

Although…it had been a long time since she'd attempted anything involving the opposite sex. Making a pass at the best man might not be the smartest thing she could do.

Even so, Whitney went with the red cashmere sweater—the kind a single, handsome man might accidentally brush with his fingers—and headed out. The house had hallways in all directions, and she was relieved when she heard voices—Jo's and Phillip's and another voice, deep and strong. Matthew.

She hurried down the steps, then remembered she was trying to make a good impression. She slowed too quickly and stumbled. Hard. She braced for the impact.

It didn't come. Instead of hitting the floor, she fell into a pair of strong arms and against a firm, warm chest.

Whitney looked up into a pair of eyes that were deep blue. He smiled down at her and she didn't feel as if she was going to forget her own name. She felt as if she'd never forget this moment.

"I've got you."

He did have her. His arms were around her waist and he was lifting her up. She felt secure.

The feeling was *wonderful*.

Then, without warning, everything changed. His warm smile froze as his eyes went hard. The strong arms became iron bars around her and the next thing she knew, she was being pushed not up, but away.

Matthew Beaumont set her back on her feet and stepped clear of her. With a glare that could only be described as ferocious, he turned to Phillip and Jo.

"What," he said, "is Whitney Wildz doing here?"

Don't miss
A BEAUMONT CHRISTMAS WEDDING
By Sarah M. Anderson

Available November 2014 from Harlequin® Desire.

HARLEQUIN®

Desire

POWERFUL HEROES... SCANDALOUS SECRETS... BURNING DESIRES!

**Explore the new tantalizing story from
the *Texas Cattleman's Club: After the Storm* series**

SHELTERED BY THE MILLIONAIRE

**by *USA TODAY* bestselling author
Catherine Mann**

As a Texas town rebuilds, love heals all wounds....

Texas tycoon Drew Farrell has always been a thorn in
Beth Andrews's side, especially when he puts the kibosh
on her animal shelter. But when he saves her daughter
during the worst tornado in recent memory, Beth sees
beneath his prickly exterior to the hero underneath.
Soon, the storm's recovery makes bedfellows of these
opposites. Until Beth's old reflexes kick in—should she
brace for betrayal or say yes to Drew once and for all?

Available **NOVEMBER 2014**
wherever books and ebooks are sold.

Talk to us online!
www.Facebook.com/HarlequinBooks
www.Pinterest.com/HarlequinBooks
www.Twitter.com/HarlequinBooks

HD733491